The Game Hunters

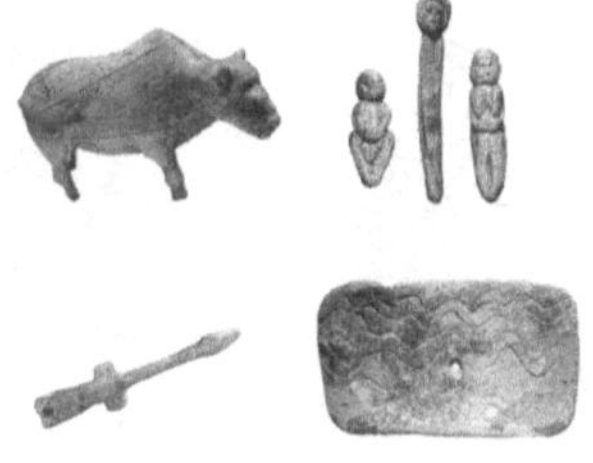

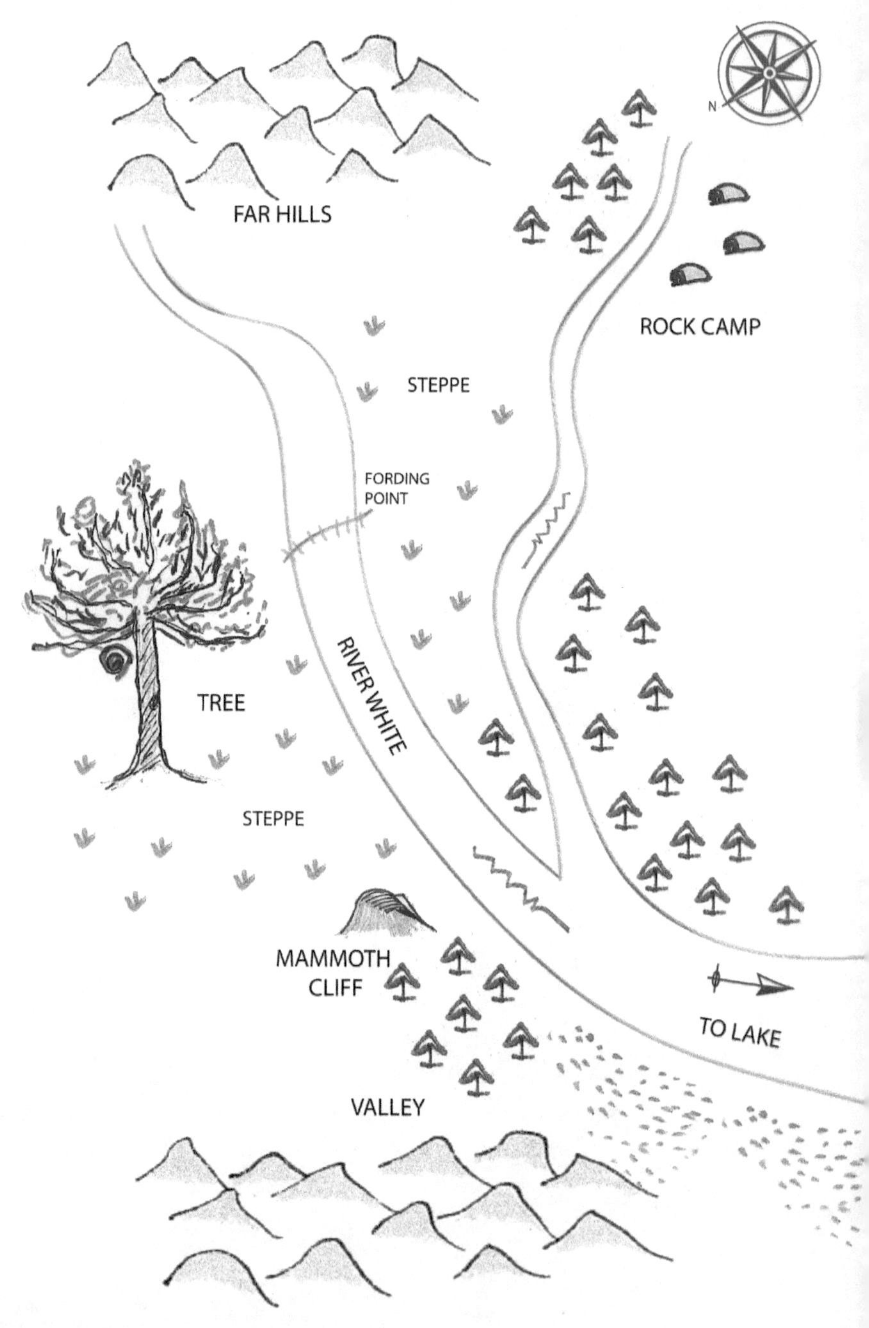

FAR HILLS
N
ROCK CAMP
STEPPE
FORDING POINT
RIVER WHITE
TREE
STEPPE
MAMMOTH CLIFF
TO LAKE
VALLEY

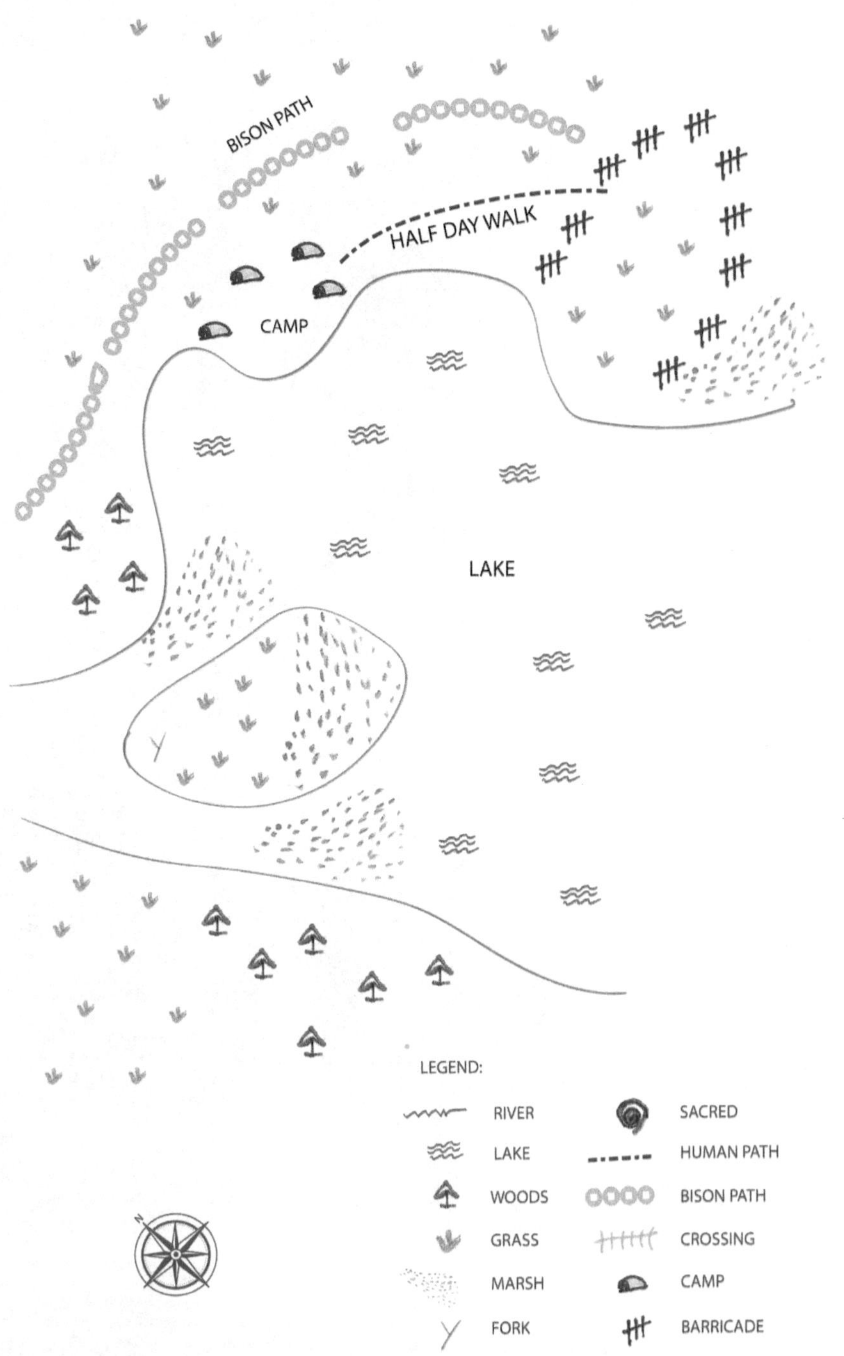

BISON PATH
HALF DAY WALK
CAMP
LAKE
LEGEND:
RIVER
LAKE
WOODS
GRASS
MARSH
FORK
SACRED
HUMAN PATH
BISON PATH
CROSSING
CAMP
BARRICADE
N

The Game Hunters

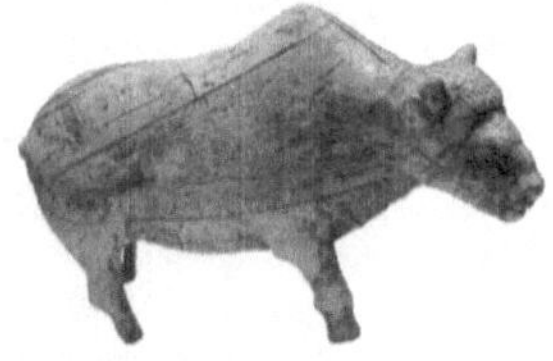

ANUPA ROY

BALESTIER PRESS
LONDON · SINGAPORE

Balestier Press
71-75 Shelton Street, London WC2H 9JQ
www.balestier.com

The Game Hunters
Copyright © Anupa Roy, 2019

First published by Balestier Press in 2019

Published with the support of

NATIONAL ARTS COUNCIL
SINGAPORE

A CIP catalogue record for this book
is available from the British Library.

ISBN 978 1 911221 30 2

To Dadu—you were my very first storyteller

And to 'the boys' for the encouragement

Contents

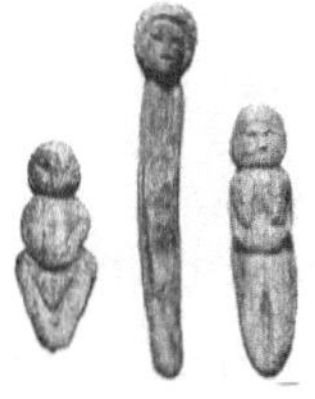

Prologue

There was great excitement in the Tribe of Healing Tree. It had been many years since the ibex had come so far north. A herd of ten was browsing on the riverbanks. People said it was lack of water which brought them down from their mountain homes.

Ibex skin had magical powers. Manuk chose the old ibex, sparing the younger ones.

Shiga saw the beautiful creatures when he went to check his traps behind Mammoth Cliff. He loved their elegant, long, ringed horns—like miniature tusks—the forgotten, yellowing mammoth tusks at the back of

Cave—where Elder tended them. He felt sadness, which one of the beautiful ibex had come to its death?

The Day of Initiation arrived. Already, the grass stood tall in the sheltered valley behind the Cliff. The sky was bright blue and the grey of Freeze was melting away leaving untidy patches of slushy snow. The tribe members had gathered on the low hill overlooking the small valley, to its north-east.

Shiga saw it all with mounting dismay. One of four initiates, he reluctantly joined in hedging the old ibex— away from the riverside and into the valley. The new grass in the valley helped. The ibex sniffed the wind then bent its head to graze, occasionally lifting it warily. The rest of the herd, nervous at the sight of so many humans had moved upstream.

Shiga and the Initiates had hidden, crouched in the scraggy dwarf fir bushes, careful to remain upwind. The ibex must believe they had left.

Sleepy in the warmth—trying not to doze or think of the ibex, a moving shadow on the valley had made him look up.

A cloud of snow geese flew together like a large spear-

head. They were on their way to Lake, to nest and fish in the warm moons. Shiga sighed and rubbed his cramped leg.

At last, Hil gave the sign. Still crouching, ever so slowly, they began to close the circle around the animal. Shiga could see its dark winter coat giving way to lighter spots of new fur. The horns curved backwards in a slight arc—thick at the base and tapering gracefully to the tip.

What a beautiful animal it was.

When they reached spear-throw distance, of a sudden he broke cover.

The ibex ran. Three pairs of eyes glared at him.

"What did you do that for?" Hil hissed like the Goddess's serpent guard, her father Manuk's grey-green eyes flashing from her face.

Shiga was glad though he hadn't planned it. It was a useless kill—though of course, the Healers prized its horns, skin and stomach. He didn't answer Hil, she would not understand; he tried to slow his pounding heart, not to clench his teeth.

He glanced towards the hill—the tribespeople

watched. That's all the hunters seemed to do, thought Shiga—watch and wait. And kill needlessly! He too set traps. But that was very different; he rarely killed anything so beautiful. He ignored the flash of red fur—the picture in the mind.

How he wished this useless Initiation was over!

At Hil's command, they once more stalked the now edgy ibex. It had reached the base of the hill, the way to the river being blocked by Watchers. The poor animal was terrified. Hil gave the signal.

Zidn hefted his spear, judging for wind direction before his throw. But he threw it just a bit late, the ibex was already scrambling up the hillside. Shiga glanced up, the tribespeople had melted away.

Hil started to climb sending loose rocks scattering down; as the surefooted ibex leapt higher, they followed.

The ibex must have sensed the tribespeople for it swerved suddenly and jumped down to the valley with Hil scrambling after it. Shiga jumped down too. For a few heartbeats, he had hoped it would escape.

The cornered ibex now lowered its head and charged Hil. Just when two man-lengths away, she threw her *spear.*

It caught the animal between the shoulder blades. Its front legs folded; its eyes looking straight at Shiga just behind her.

Shiga clenched his fists to curb the rising panic. Zidn, slow to come down, now ran ahead to put a spear through its heart, stilling the suffering animal. The blood flowed.

Shiga looked away. Up on the hill Manuk was speaking to Gath. With a curt nod, Gath left the group.

Shiga forced himself to breathe, to look at the ibex laid on its side. The Initiates were tying its legs with thongs. Blood seeped into the ground; staining the yellow and blue grass flowers. It would not be long before the bees, the midgets and gnats hovered over the flowers, thought Shiga.

He turned and walked away to the wood near the river, his new spear swinging loosely in his hand.

Why couldn't they leave him alone to get on with his tools?

That night he dreamt again of the bison head.

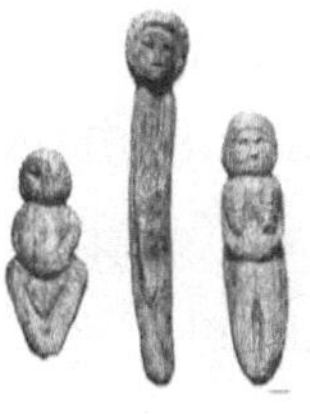

1

Land of Ice

Shiga stomped on last night's layer of snow. The pre-dawn blue grudgingly gave way to a soft golden glow. The vast land shimmered white. Out on the cold, windy overhang since dawn, he wondered what was keeping Urm? Unless she was talking to Bruj. Shiga went red and stomped again. Below him, River White was on its way to Lake, a mass of deep blue water, white foam and ice, carrying bleached logs and floes whirling on its frothy waters.

Bruj was everywhere, grasping and meddling in everything! Just before dawn, when he had woken in a sweat, staring at the smouldering embers of Gath's hearth, trying to shake off that terrible dream, Bruj had been watching him!

"Afraid?" his low mutter had startled Shiga. Gritting his teeth, Shiga had grabbed his cape and hurried out of the warm cave of sleeping bodies. How he would have liked to hit Bruj—just once—but one did not hit a guest! He would not upset the tribe anymore.

It was two years since he had failed his initiation; two years since he had dreamt the dream. Yet last night was the third in a row. Shiga hugged himself against the cold wind. Why now, when Tribe Mother had trusted him with Fat Gathering.

He turned his face to the warmth from the east, sunlight was creeping onto the overhang, soon it would reach the outer Cave. He looked towards Tree, ancient and eternal—now leafless. He took a deep breath to let in air and sun into his heart and lungs—to let in the blessings of Tree.

Upstream, beyond Tree, White's waters churned

around the boulders of Fording Point as if daring one to cross it. But soon its flow would gentle; other tribesmen would cross and it would be time for First Hunt. Manuk had made it clear that Shiga didn't have a choice this time.

The dream was the last thing he wanted now.

The dream had made him cry as a child—the half-severed head and horns, the burly man with the axe, hacking, hacking… in a river of blood! Tribe Mother had soothed him even though he had never spoken of it! Shiga rubbed his forehead as if to erase the image.

Tree's bare branches shook gently.

The winds whipped his light brown hair against his face and blew off his hood, but it had lost the bite of the Freeze moons. He drew in another deep lungful, loving the whiteness and silence. The land of Sibur—harsh, cold but oh—so beautiful.

Soon would come the Growing—first tufts and patches of grass, then flowers. For a few full moons, the land would wear the Goddess' green mantle. Tree would too.

The herds of bison or musk ox would arrive,

following the river towards Lake. And the killing would begin—turning the green land red! This year he had to be one of the killers—this year and every year.

Shiga squared his shoulders and started to climb down the boulder-steps. Urm would have to follow—but she was right, he saw too much inside his head.

Dear Urm. Already, word of her healing skills and beauty had spread to the tribes, Shiga knew it wasn't only Bruj who would seek her company at the Meeting after First Hunt, when the Tribe Mothers would announce the Joinings. What chance would he stand—one who had seen fifteen Growings already—and not hunted with the men? Bruj lost no chances to point that out—but always out of the hearing of others.

Bruj and Ina had arrived a year ago—Bruj to learn from Gath—best toolmaker of all tribes and Shiga's adopted father and hero. Ina to be a healer under Duni; for the tribe of Wolf had eager hunters but no Healer since their last one died.

From the first Bruj had refused his friendship. Shiga knew no one had said anything about him, but such news travelled. Besides he had skipped First Hunt last year. It made him cringe inside. At least after the Hunt, they would be rid of Bruj.

But what of himself? Where would he be?

Perhaps Urm preferred Bruj…

Shiga caught himself from slipping forcing his wandering mind back; the sun's warmth was turning the ice slippery. The hilly stretches far to the south and east were just becoming visible through the distant mist. It wasn't wise to leave the dead bison-calf unguarded, the Tree Guardians had returned before dawn.

Urm's shout made him stop. He turned to see her hurrying down. Tribe Mother had come out with Nes on the overhang where he had stood a while ago.

Urm slid over a boulder and landed next to him with a grunt.

"You're very late," he admonished.

"Mother's last minute instructions. You know how she gets before the Ceremony." Urm whispered.

"Wondered if you'd forgotten, Protector of Grasses."

A shove sent him scrambling downwards flapping his hands. At the bottom, he waved to the older women.

* * *

"May the Blessings of Goddess Mother and Tree be on them," intoned Tribe Mother, watching the two. As leader, she must have no favourites; but Urm was her own daughter and Shiga had come to her at three, when his parents died of the breathing disease for which she still had no healing. She had been Chief Healer before Duni. So she had done what was always done—taken the orphan child into the healers' hearth. It felt so long ago.

"Hunters prefer Shiga's spear-heads over their own. And his traps never fail." Nes' slow voice broke into her thoughts.

"Yes, and always so helpful... If only..." Tribe Mother sighed.

"If only he would hunt." Nes finished. The women fell quiet.

Even as a toddler, Shiga would wander over to Gath's hearth and sit patiently watching the toolmakers. Gath had humoured the four-year-old giving him a blunt chisel and small bones to play with. Shiga started following him everywhere. Gath with no child of his own was protective.

At six, Shiga had shown Gath his first spear-head, delighting the man and surprising the tribespeople. Gath began to teach the boy, he made a pendant of that first spear-head and hung it around Shiga's neck. Shiga still wore it.

"He will make a hunter—in time," said Tribe Mother. Manuk had mentioned the old laws. She shivered.

"It is two years since… last year too, he disappeared before First Hunt." Nes spoke gently, but a frown gathered her eyebrows. "The other tribes will ask questions. If only—he at least joined the Hunt!" she kept what Manuk had said to herself. When Shiga disappeared, the other huntsmen were upset and had spoken of the old laws.

"I tried talking to him," Tribe Mother said wearily, "he… only stared at the cave-floor."

Manuk had been furious; Shiga had broken the laws and even when he had convinced Nad to let the boy join First Hunt, he had disappeared shaming him and the tribe! The Elders had decided to give Shiga one more chance. But even she—Tribe Mother of Healing Tree couldn't prevent the tribes from invoking the ancient law. The Tribes came first and her's was always looked up to—they were the oldest in the land. As the Growing neared, her nights had turned sleepless.

"I will soften Manuk" said Nes and went in to the Cave. But it wasn't about Manuk, they both knew.

Tribe Mother looked into the distance, where the sun was just sending the mists away. Like dust behind a pack of fleeing horses. When had the last horse pack come this way? How many Growings!

How fast the seasons turned. She remembered Urm's father, Chief Huntsman before Manuk. He had died so young, so soon after their joining, she herself barely older than her Urm. Now she could not even remember his face. Just a gored, dying man she had tried desperately to heal. And failed.

Urm did not even remember his face! And Tribe Mother never took another mate. From Healer to Tribe Mother—she had always put the Tribe above all else. Would she have to cast Shiga out? It would break her heart!

The children were now little dots on the white and grey landscape.

Urm was a fast learner, said Duni. At thirteen she was growing beautiful too. But the girl believed plants could be grown, not just gathered! As if she was Goddess Mother herself! When she had found out, her heart had filled with fear.

"Hush! That is the work of the Goddess!"

"It is food Mother. The Goddess will not be offended, sure." Urm was so confident!

Tribe Mother was thankful no one knew about it yet. The tribes only gathered what was grown and given by the Goddess. That was how it always had been.

But times were getting harder, the cold got worse every Freeze. Horse herds were unseen, the mammoths had vanished even before her time.

And there were fewer plants to gather. People died often! Thank the Goddess, their tribe had lost no one this last Freeze. They had just enough food, but she feared for the future. If the tribe was to survive, it would need new skills.

A boy who refused to hunt and a girl who believed she possessed the Divine power! Was that the answer? "Oh Goddess Mother send me signs," she prayed.

2

Fat Gathering

Urm and Shiga sloshed their way avoiding the bigger puddles, those were dangerous, where one could fall deep and break a leg.

A deep puddle. That's exactly what the Initiation felt like, thought Shiga; a deep puddle he had stepped into and could not get out of.

Urm was looking closely to see which trees had survived Freeze. Last Growing, four larches, had sent out thin shoots from their earthy homes; before Freeze she had collected flotsam and pieces of bone and hide to build a guard around the young saplings. These were now broken, mostly blown away by the winds. But the saplings lived. They would grow slowly, their roots stubbornly clutching the riverbank .

"Wish they were willows," she pointed the saplings out to Shiga.

He nodded. A few alders sheltered humbly behind boulders along the riverbank, for warmth. Closer to the water, bold grasses and sedges had begun to put out their shoots.

"Would it matter—if I was sent away?" Shiga's voice was nonchalant.

Urm's head jerked up— her eyes, glistening. "Manuk says in earlier times, initiates were sent out during the Growing. Alone!"

"Mostly they went in twos or threes. If they returned in seven suns with a straight kill, they were accepted," he knew the stories. "But yes, sometimes they went alone. Often they didn't return."

"It's cruel," burst out Urm.

"Hunting is cruel too."

Urm nodded, confused. "You will not be sent … not after First Hunt." She didn't want to think of it. Shiga never spoke of hunts and she never asked. She wished she knew what bothered him; at least he was ready to speak, something he hadn't done for two years! Not to her or anyone else. The whole tribe waited to see if he would hunt this time!

"Bruj is a good hunter, they tell," he had to know what she thought of Bruj.

Urm glared at him, "Hurry, we don't have all day to discuss a wolf whelp!" she briskly walked ahead. Is that what bothered him? Bruj seemed to bring out the worst in Shiga. And she hated the way Bruj was seeking her out more and more these days; even Mother had asked her what she thought of him! She tried to be polite But the boy sneered behind people's backs—even at Manuk! Sometimes she thought the elders were blind!

"Initiation hunts have become simpler," Shiga mimicked Elder of River Hearth—the oldest of the tribes—no one remembered his name.

Urm's laughter swept over him, like the first warm winds over the land. His heaviness lifted.

"Actually lazy you should live on your own. Without us reminding you about meals when you carve!" Urm matched Shiga's changing mood.

"All right, that saves me a few hare furs then. You can make yourself a coat of leaves for next Freeze," Shiga laughed.

Though he knew she was pretty good at net-hunting herself! But Shiga always saved the best hare and fox furs for her.

Shiga caught up with Urm and spun her around. Righting her balance quickly over the slippery ice, she smacked him.

"Sometime I wonder if you are a tree-spirit," he teased.

"I turn into one at night," she made a face.

Shiga smiled, First Hunt would need all his will to go through. But Urm was there.

As if echoing his thoughts Urm now asked, "Shiga, when you go to First Hunt, will you bury some seeds on Lakeshore for me? And will you check if there are any bulrushes growing near …"

Shiga rolled his eyes skywards. "It is a Hunt! If anyone sees me, they will think I am touched!" then looking serious, "Will you not anger the Goddess?"

"I don't think so," Urm's words were slow—Shiga *was* going to hunt this time, if only she could be sure. Perhaps if the Goddess allowed her to grow Her plants, they need not hunt so much! And animals got scarcer every year! But if Shiga didn't hunt—the old laws would be invoked—she had overheard Nes whispering to Duni.

Oh Goddess Mother, let Shiga hunt this time! Perhaps Mother had chosen Shiga for Fat Gathering for a reason—Urm had to be content with that!

"What a long talk Manuk gave me after—the … the ibex. And Gath refused to talk for months," Shiga forced out the words. Urm paused in her stride, then continued. He had never talked of the Initiation— until now. That was a good sign.

"It was after ten suns and two good spear-heads I made, that Gath spoke to me, 'Not even Manuk can hunt big game alone. We work together, watching out for each other. There is always the chance of an accident.'"

Urm peered at Shiga's face from under her hood, and squeezed his arm. Was he afraid of being wounded, then? Her heart skipped, hunters were careful but there were injuries.

"Big game brings us food. Without it no one will survive Freeze. And taking a life is always … difficult" Urm spoke softly. He was not averse to trapping smaller game, in fact she had taught him the best way to make hunting nets that wouldn't tear.

"Oh yes, yes—heard it—many times," Shiga quickened his pace.

Urm sighed—so touchy he had become this last year!

"Do you think the antelopes will come this Growing?" she asked after a while.

"No, it will probably be bison—like last year."

"Antelopes, are tastier."

"Antelopes have gone south, it's warmer there," he wondered what it would be like to follow the antelope herds to the warm south. Perhaps if he had to leave— he would go south.

"What if the bison too go south?" Urm had to quicken her pace to keep up, how tall Shiga was, his strides were longer than her's. Somehow in the confines of Cave she hadn't noticed.

"Not yet."

Urm's heart lifted. She would offer a special prayer to Goddess Mother—for Shiga's safe hunt.

* * *

A trail of congealed blood ran from the riverbank to Tree, where the calf had been dragged. It lay red-black against the white snow. Manuk had killed the calf two suns before. It had wandered away from its herd and reached the river thirsty and frightened. And to its death, thought Shiga.

The scarecrow—a fox-skull on an antler lodged into the ground, swayed in the breeze.

On the sturdier branches of Tree, three man-lengths high, hung the Healers' Hut. Built of the Tree's own branches and some bones, it was used by the Healers and Tribe Mother when they wanted to commune with the Goddess. And it was said the spirit of Tree often lived there.

Last two nights, along with the two Tree Guardians, they had watched from the overhang to ensure no hyenas or wolves got wind of the dead calf— in daylight the scarecrow did its job well.

Yesterday Tribe Mother had announced the Lighting of the Lamp.

Setting down their bags Urm and Shiga circled Tree thrice. Then they set to the task.

Shiga gritted his teeth as each dipped their right-hand fingers in the congealed blood of the calf's innards. It felt he had thrust his hand into the gory bison head of his dreams. His teeth clenched; Urm put a hand on his shoulder as if to steady herself. Shiga let out his breath.

They drew the signs of the Tribe, the Ceremony and the bison spirit on the ancient bark of Tree. With faded signs of earlier years covering its bole, Tree was a witness to generations of Fat-gathering. Shiga kept his eyes on Tree. She calmed him.

Urm made ready the thin small sacks of ibex intestines, careful not to damage the precious bags. The same ibex which Shiga had refused to hunt. There had been no more ibex after that.

Holding his breath he cut away the fat from the inner

hide with his paring stone and made lumps of it on the snow. It was cold and hard—he rarely gutted the small game he hunted—so many were eager to claim them!

Urm sat scooping the fat with a slat of fox bone into the bags. As she filled each one, she pulled close its drawstring of dried tendon and put it carefully into a big hide bag. They collected six bags of fat.

At last Shiga stood up keeping his hands away from his body. It was done! The rest would be collected later. And every bit of fat from it would burn in Her lamps. This calf was sacred, to be returned to the Goddess; the carcass must be thrown to the river, for the fishes. Only after the Hunt would they collect fat and bones for their own use.

"Let's get back," he longed to wash his hands and the splatter of gore on his tunic. Approaching noon, the whiteness of the ice was blinding. Shading her eyes, Urm looked to the east where black specks moved like soot fallen on ice.

"The Scouters are looking for signs of the herd."

Shiga grunted intent on cleaning his hands with a piece of old hare fur.

Urm looked longingly at the river, "Think we could wash there?"

He glanced at the rushing waters and then at Mammoth Cliff. There was no one on the ledge but with the ice dazzling his eyes, he couldn't be sure.

"Too dangerous, besides we don't go to the river before the Ceremony. You know that." But the waters looked very tempting.

"Near the boulder, the water is calmer." Urm pretended she had not heard.

Shiga looked at his blood-stained hands. It would be nice to wash them clean, really clean. Throughout the long Freeze they made do with melted ice. He was longing for a good bath in the river. Not for another few days! The river was still dangerous. Absently, he ran a hand around the back of his neck, then grimaced at the sticky fat and blood on it.

"A quick wash then. But you stay close." There was a reason they were forbidden—River White was at her trickiest at Melting—it could carry one away, or dash one to pieces against the rocks at the bend of Cliff.

They had to be very careful. And they *must* not be seen.

* * *

They stepped carefully down to the water's edge, keeping a wary eye on the cliff. The ground was very slippery and slushy. Boulders lay strewn; where the river made a slight bend, was the largest one. Flat on top, its sides worn smooth by the high waters of many floods, this was a place the children loved. Here, between the bank and the boulder the waters flowed more quietly.

They had removed their outer trousers and coats and laid them out on the bank. As they rolled up their leggings of rhino wool, the cold hit their bare legs. Shivering they waded, ankle deep.

"Ooh!" Urm cried out as the ice-melt waters numbed her legs.

"Sh..sh..shut up." Shiga chattered through his teeth as he glanced fearfully towards the Cliff now half hidden behind the boulder.

"Ca…can't he—he…help, it's so cold. And lovely."

Shiga glared at her recklessness. Urm grinned. She bent down carefully and began to splash water over her face and neck. The water at her feet swirled but the rocks prevented the river's angry rush from sweeping them off.

Shiga dug his feet into the pebbles beneath, leaning against the rock. Even as he bent down to wash, he kept an eye on Urm.

It felt wonderful. The ice-melt washed away the stiffness and the grime.

The sun was bright and slanted across the river turning the frothy waters into glinting shells, like the ones around Urm's neck. Shiga thought she was so like the river—lively and uncaring.

"C'mon back," he said.

In an eye-blink she splashed him laughing at his startled look.

"Stop that Urm." Grinning he held up his hands, then made a sudden grab and dragged her up the bank.

Chilled and wet, they quickly wore their outer clothes. "I think I will have to give this away." Urm looked down at her wet leggings, now shrunk tight against her calves. Gathering was a good time to exchange gifts.

"You are as fat as the bison calf," laughed Shiga, ducking her blow. But he noticed how elegant and strong her legs were.

Urm chased him all the way to Tree. As they stood panting, a figure came out to the overhang.

"That was close," he knew it was too far to see what they were doing but sounds carried and he was glad they had come away from the river. He frowned at his wet clothes.

"Stop worrying, they will dry before we reach."

"And give me a chill."

The walk back was difficult. Their wet clothes felt horribly uncomfortable. More of the snow had melted.

Shiga looked up at Mammoth Cliff—home to their tribe for generations. People said it was aptly named. Twelve man-lengths high, it sloped down to the broad ledge overhang and hid their home well; from there down to the narrow river bank, the slope was steeper. At this distance it looked just like a mammoth—at least how he'd heard they looked—round cave-head, with a steeply sloping ridge-back to the river.

Nearing the Cliff, they saw Nes.

"Wasn't it fun," Urm whispered back.

"Yes, but I can't afford any more trouble."

"Am I trouble?" Urm stopped in mid-stride, her eyes dancing. A dimple caught in her chin and her wet half-dry hair shone brilliantly.

Shiga's breath caught, he looked away. Was this what the Goddess would look like if he saw Her? He could not let Bruj take her away—not if he were to die at First Hunt!

3

Lighting of the Lamp

Sitting cross-legged, with her back to the entrance, Tribe Mother stared intently into the flames. The firelight brought out the deep crimson of her Ceremonial Robe.

All fifteen tribe members sat around Mother Hearth, the same red reflected in the hunt-bands on their foreheads. Shiga sat at the back, proud that the fox pelts on Tribe Mother's robe and the foxtail hunt-bands that the tribespeople wore, were mostly from his traps. It was pleasant and warm in the inner cave.

The ancient mammoth-ivory lamps glowed in the firelight, the bags of fat gathered that morning resting beside them. Urm and Duni, their faces red as the fox pelts moved hot stones out of the fire with long forked branches. A burning bone cracked loudly. Tribe Mother looked up and caught Shiga's eye, she gave a slight nod. He smiled. As her foster-son, he belonged to the Mother Hearth. It felt good.

"Thank the Goddess for her grace. We have not lost anyone to Freeze." Tribe Mother's voice was calm and deep, as she looked around at the gathered tribe.

"Thank the Goddess," intoned the tribespeople, Shiga's voice mingling with theirs.

A long shadow fell across the wall; it settled itself just behind him. It whispered—"Move over, little boy."

Shiga felt himself turn red. Hil next to him frowned. How dare Bruj … Shiga nearly missed the next chant and forced himself to focus.

"It is Melting Time, our Mother the Earth Goddess is coming to life." Tribe Mother's voice rumbled—as if rising from the very depths of the rock floor.

"The Goddess is coming to life." Like a waterfall the sound of all their voices rang around the cave walls. The flames flickered and leapt, threw quick shadows before settling again.

Duni signalled to Urm and Tami. They laid hot stones in triangles of three all around the hearth. Red-orange fur mittens protected them. A familiar ceremony but this year Shiga felt a strange stirring inside him. This year he would hunt the big game and ask the Elders permission to join Urm.

Tribe Mother rose, then circled the fire calling on its grace to light their way; she placed an ivory lamp on each of the five triangles. One for each of the five tribes.

Tami and Urm scooped out fat from the ibex skin bags—the fat that he had gathered—and placed some in each lamp. As it melted with the heat, Duni quickly inserted the wicks of dried lichen. The lamps were ready.

Urm's face was flushed, droplets of sweat like dew on her forehead. Had she always looked so beautiful, so distant. Shiga could not move his eyes from her.

"May the lamps be lighted," Manuk's deep gruff voice spoke for all the tribesmen.

"If the Goddess Mother wishes it," answered Tribe Mother.

One by one she lit the lamps with the reindeer-antler torch. At its fiery end burnt dry lichen tied in strips of old hides soaked in fat. Everyone had stood up.

Shiga stood with them—he belonged to the best tribe of all, and Urm was the best of them—he would not disappoint them at First Hunt.

"Fire has lighted our lamps, warmed us in Freeze moons; fire softened our food and warmed our children. It is time to feed Fire." Tribe Mother's voice resounded against Cave's walls and the high dark ceiling and seemed to become one with the hill—as if it was the very Spirit of the Goddess.

She poured melted fat onto the fire. Fed, it splattered and rose high. Those nearest stepped back as from an angry animal.

Then it was time for them; one by one they went up to the fire—scooping up a little bison-fat and dropping it into the blaze. First went Manuk.

The fire now spluttering and hissing reflected strange shapes off Cave's high roof. Each time the tribespeople chanted, 'We thank Fire and we thank Goddess Mother.'

The Ceremony was a job of honour that their tribe performed every year for all five tribes.

It was Shiga's turn. Before he could reach the fire, Bruj stepped in front of him—Shiga caught his breath—forced to stop short. He watched, furious— as Bruj swaggered up—he saw Duni's eyes narrow and Tribe Mother's momentary frown. He waited for his missed turn trying to ignore the amused looks and Bruj's contemptuous smirk as he returned.

As Shiga went up, the hide curtain drawn close for the night swung open—an icy gust entered the cave. The flames swung wildly, then dwindled. Startled, Shiga stopped with the fat scoop in his hand. Moving quickly, Bruj caught the curtain and drew it close, weighing it down with a large rock. There were approving nods.

The fire burnt steadily again, but the warmth inside had gone.

Shiga finished to a hasty chant feeling cheated.

"It's time to choose the Hunt Maiden," announced Manuk, bringing back everyone's attention.

Tribe Mother opened her fist to show the clay model, then threw it into the fire—she stepped back watching it closely. The soft wet clay cracked with a loud pop and Duni fished it out. It would tell the Hunt Maiden's name and tribe; then she would be sent for. It was a great honour to be Hunt Maiden.

Lifting her eyes from the blackened clay doll, Tribe Mother pointed to Urm!

"It is her—Urm the Hunt Maiden."

Shiga's chest tightened, he could no longer breathe.

He watched in a daze. Manuk walked over and was bowing low to Urm—the Hunt Maiden was revered. He saw Urm's bewildered face. As Maiden of the Hunt, she would accompany the chosen hunters to the Ceremony!

But he would not be chosen—he was not a hunter, not even an initiate!

It was as if he stood very far away—watching people

he knew nothing about. A strange discomfort trickled down his spine. He didn't belong! He was a failure. Even if he hunted this year, he was no match for Urm Healer and Hunt Maiden!

"A very pretty Hunt Maiden. Don't you think?" Shiga didn't need to turn—he would know Bruj's grating voice anywhere.

He nodded. Bruj was right—for once. Urm was the most beautiful Hunt Maiden ever chosen by the Goddess!

"Will you be going to—oh I forget!" Bruj covered his face in mock embarrassment, then muttered, "Cast-offs don't survive long."

Shiga whirled round but Bruj was walking away. Shiga felt his feet had turned to stone.

Someone took up a flute and started a quick tune. Soon the beat of a drum joined it—low and soft. The sombre mood changed to talk and laughter. Dried meat and roasted grass seeds were being passed around. Shiga made for the cave entrance.

Bruj was leaning against the wall next to the store in the outer cave. Other young hunters stood around talking. Roni and Tami were offering them food; all hunters would be treated specially till they left. Not he though. An adopted son of Tribe Mother, he was to be tolerated till they were ready to cast him out.

Tribe Mother may have worn his fox pelts—the whole tribe may love the furs he gave them—but he was not one of them—who was he! It was pity they all felt. And Urm treated everyone kindly. Loud laughter rose behind like a wall of ridicule.

Shiga stood at the very edge of the overhang, looking out over the darkened landscape, where that very morning he had stood in hope. The cold mist rising from the river soon enveloped him. His face began to grow numb.

*　*　*

Inside, Urm went to her mother. "What do I have to do as Maiden?"

Tribe Mother was taking off her red robe. She looked ordinary now, like any other woman and tired; she smiled. Each time the Maiden of the Hunt needed reassurance before the secret Ceremony.

This year she was anxious too, only she could never

show it. Choosing the Hunt Maiden was not a decision she took lightly, she hoped it was the right one; the success of the Hunt depended on it.

"You will know when it is time," she said, just as she told each Maiden, every year. Then her eyes looking troubled, "And you cannot speak with … with non-initiates till the Ceremony," she felt a pang.

Urm stared then turned away, her eyes searching—where was Shiga? Wasn't he allowed to congratulate her even? The worry which had eased in the morning, returned—what would happen if Shiga did not hunt this year. She would have to speak to him! Whatever Mother said. May the Goddess forgive her!

It was as if they were being pulled apart by unseen hands.

The tribespeople laughed and joked and congratulated Urm. She tried to answer, to smile but her mind was a whirl. Shiga wasn't in the Caves. As soon as she could, Urm hurried to peer outside.

A cold sliver of a moon glinted off the stone water-bowl; and a dark shape stood alone in the bone-chilling mist.

She wrapped her robe a little tighter and walked out. The wind had dropped.

Shiga heard her, 'Congratulations Hunt Maiden!' He did not turn.

Why was it that the same word could sound so different when spoken by different people, thought Urm.

"Shiga come in from the cold. You'll be sick."

"Well a cast-out has to get used to cold!"

"Stop it Shiga! You will not be cast out."

"No?" he gave a dry laugh. She tried to lay a hand on his arm, he jerked away.

"Why are you here, Hunt Maiden? Your place is with the hunters!" the brittleness of the words made Urm gasp.

"Shiga, I did not choose to be Hunt Maiden."

"You were chosen—as you will be again—by another!"

"If you mean Bruj—I do not even like him. And I don't think Mother will …"

"Anyway after First Hunt, all this—"

Shiga turned towards her—the firelight glowered in his pupils.

"Go—to the hunters; why are you here with non-initiate!" he spat out.

Urm turned away but not before he'd seen her tears.

Snatches of laughter, talk and that awful trill of the flute spilled out to be gobbled by the darkness. Gusts of wind froze his face; Freeze liked to remind of its ubiquitous presence. Shiga stood—he was not just a coward but mean. He didn't belong—perhaps he should leave now. Urm was better off with Bruj. And he felt a deep shame and hopelessness.

It was some time later that Duni came to find him half-frozen in the cold. Scolding, she forced him to come in and gave him a hot bone broth. People were settling in for the night. Shiga had a splitting headache; Duni, who noticed everything gave him medicine tea, to ease the throbbing. Her hand was cool on his forehead—"Keep your anger for First Hunt," she murmured.

Shiga crept into the farthest corner of Cave and lay down to sleep.

Urm watched him go. As the entire cave turned quiet, she lay awake. What did a Hunt Maiden do? Tami had been Hunt Maiden last year but the Ceremony was never spoken of. Shiga had been so unkind. And now she couldn't speak to him! Rules, rules!

And Bruj—even this evening he had cornered her, smiling, so sure that she liked him!

She wished the hunters would leave—with their swaggering and bravado. Their work was important but so was gathering and net hunting. So much fuss they made over it!

If only her plans succeeded!

If only Shiga hunted this time. But did he even care for her? All her confidence of the morning washed away in tears, soaking the bed-furs around her neck.

4

The Ceremony

For five suns from the Lighting of the Lamp, every dawn and dusk the mammoth drum beat summoned the tribes. The Melt had set in well, River White allowed itself to be crossed with care.

People from tribes of Wolf, Horse and Far Hill arrived—Chief huntsmen, senior hunters and the healer of Tribe of Far Hill, sister to Urm's mother. Five tribes hunted the big game together. Lake tribespeople rarely came for the Ceremony, their totem of the snow-geese carried by Tribe Mother, represented them.

Thirteen people winded their way in single file

through the labyrinths. Tribe Mother led the way with Manuk. Bruj followed closely. The Hunt Maiden brought up the end of the procession with her aunt. All the women carried lamps and the men spears.

Urm stared at the tall shadows on the narrow passage walls and ceiling, bending over them, ushering them into the Otherworld. The tunnel sloped deeper and deeper into the earth. Did it lead all the way to the abode of Goddess Mother.

Footsteps echoed behind. She looked over her shoulder but gripping her arm, her aunt hurried her along. On and on, down, down into the very bowels of the hill; she had never known this place existed.

It was strangely eerie walking in the semi-dark—torchlights throwing weird shadows! Goddess Mother, this was Her abode, Urm curbed her thoughts!

Her throat scratched, she swallowed to hold back a cough.

The women wore hooded capes, their heads covered in tightly woven caps, looking like Helpers—those sisters of the Mother Goddess who were her eyes and ears, and who took serpent forms, living in the depths of earth. Urm shivered and glanced at the shadows snaking along with them.

The men's faces were painted with the sacred red-earth.

Her arm began to throb, Urm loosened it from her aunt's grip but kept in step.

Like shadows of the Otherworld they walked on. She didn't notice when they had started to chant but suddenly the sound filled her mind—had she ever heard anything so beautiful and frightening at the same time. When the women's voices fell away, the men's rose in crescendo. The sound magnified, rung against the stone walls. Echoes and shadows mingled. Urm drew in a ragged breath.

Were they to walk and chant all night.

Suddenly, they stopped, Urm bumping into the woman ahead. The close shadows retreated to the far walls and were barely visible. They were in a wide chamber. And then Urm nearly jumped!

A soft keening chant rose from the depths—note

after note, the voices deeper, the words unclear. Urm gripped her aunt—it was the Helpers!

The women started to hum.

Voices rose to a shrill till she wanted to cover her ears, the drumming increased; her heartbeats in rhythm with the drums.

Then the deep call of a bison filled the air!

Looking around in the dim light, Urm noticed a hunter twirling an object—the sound was from a bullroarer! Urm peered, she'd only heard of bullroarers, never seen one! It was forbidden—a powerful gift from the Goddess to hunters—to call the animals to First Hunt.

It was Shiga who told her of bullroarers—how she wished he was here! Thinking of their quarrel made her miserable, but she had no time to brood.

Low at first, then louder it sounded as if a large bison herd was approaching; single calls grew into many just as grazing bison call to each other. The hairs on Urm's arms stood on end.

Four huntsmen stepped out of the group, each lighting a flaming torch. Light flashed up as if it at a

Hunt-feast.

Urm's mouth fell open. All around her on the walls of the cave there were animal drawings.

Bison, aurochs, horses—sacred mammoths now so rarely seen. On the left wall a long-toothed fearsome cave lion was in mid-pounce on an auroch. They seemed to come out of the walls and dance in the quivering torchlight.

Line after line of animals ran—pursued by unseen hunters. Here and there one lay writhing on the ground with spears bristling from its body, its life blood spilling out.

A hunter stepped out towards a large bison charging from the right wall. He started to draw over the old red lines with a charcoal. Next to it, he drew a bison-calf—just like the one whose fat they had gathered.

Another joined him and started to draw thin lines—Urm realized it was River White; a woman to her left was drawing a huge perch in the river—its dark skin dotted. One after another men and women stepped up and joined the painters. More bison appeared on the walls, overlapping the old animals.

Soon there was an entire herd—the bullroarers twirled and the underground chamber rang with bison calls, the neighing of a horse, the cry of a bison just pierced.

The chanting continued.

An arm pulled her back for fascinated, Urm had moved very close to the painters.

The chanting stopped. Only bison calls echoed around the chamber now, softer.

A woman turned her around and began to daub red-earth on her face. She felt the warmth of the red ochre on her cheek bones. She found herself in the centre, it was time for the Hunt Maiden—but Urm had no idea what she was to do.

"No!" her cry was lost in the animal calls and echoes. Urm resisted as she was pressed down to the cave-floor!

Frantically, she looked for her Mother or aunt. Where were they? She bit her lips to choke a scream!

The floor was like ice blocks. Her teeth started to chatter. Tribespeople loomed over her like Helpers to take her to the Otherworld. Urm struggled but hands pinned her down.

"Be still," someone whispered.

Urm tried to think clearly—Tami had returned from the Ceremony. Hunt Maidens always returned unharmed. Her heart hammered but she forced herself to breathe and felt the terror subside.

But in that moment she realized what a hunted animal must feel!

The chanting had started again, Urm focused on their warm Cave home above and on Shiga; poor Shiga, he understood what the animals felt! She remembered what Tami had whispered before they left—"It will be all right."

The hunters stepped nearer. Their spear-heads glinted in the torchlight. Terrified, Urm struggled to sit up, then suddenly, her Mother's cool hand was on her forehead. Urm stopped struggling, shut her eyes. Her heart thudded along with the soft drumbeat.

She felt their footsteps circling, closing in, hemming her, paralyzing her mind. What terror a hunted animal felt!

"Has the Hunt begun," the women began to chant.

"The Hunt has begun," came the answer.

"What is our game."

"Bison is our game."

There was a pause.

"Are the lamps lighted."

"They are lighted."

"Has the fire been fed."

"The fire is fed. Goddess Mother has sent us food."

Silence. Even the drumbeat had stopped.

Urm let out her breath, her back was frozen. Then someone yelled, "Then let the hunt begin."

Like many voices the sound ricocheted in that low ceilinged, cave deep in the hill. The echoes skittered around repeating—HUNT BEGIN—HUNT BEGIN!

With a deafening cry hunters hurled themselves towards her. Urm screamed, she struggled to sit up, to run, but the hands still pinned her down. Urm screwed up her eyes expecting the spear stabs.

Then a bison cried out in mortal pain—it was a bullroarer again but she could have sworn it was a real bison!

"Goddess Mother we bring you the bison girl—the

Hunt Maiden. Bless our Hunt. We take and we give."

Urm peered through half-closed eyes—spears bristled all around—inches from her body!

"We take and we give," said the voices.

"We take and we give," rose a loud chant.

Was it just after or a long time later, Urm had no idea: a hand helped her rise. Her knees shook. The chanting was unceasing, jumbling her thoughts.

She was led away from that chamber—back, back through the long tunnels—it seemed terribly long—Urm stumbled between them; sweat poured from her forehead, her neck was wet and cold, her body burning. A woman pressed a pouch of water to her lips. She swallowed the cold liquid in gulps. And then she was back.

At the Healer's Hearth Duni was giving her another drink. This time it was warm and her mouth tasted the calming yellow poppy in it.

A small voice whispered she was not to speak of the Ceremony—ever.

She could not tell Shiga that she understood—but then they were not speaking! He would soon leave for

First Hunt—and then—she was too exhausted!

Mother always said the Tribe came first. Did it? Even before Duni wiped the paint off her face, Urm had fallen into an exhausted sleep.

* * *

No one saw them return just as no one had seen them go—except that Shiga had been unable to sleep in a corner of the cold outer cave where he had banished himself.

One by one he had seen dark shapes walk into the store next to it. And disappear! Urm, Manuk, Tribe Mother and others. And Bruj had walked with Tribe Mother—in the lead! He had to clench his teeth to prevent himself from crying his protest.

Perhaps that was the son she wanted, not a coward. Not one who asked stupid questions about the animals instead of hunting. And anyway Urm was not even talking to him anymore; why would she?

When he was sure the last person had gone—he had let the tears come.

He had failed! He did not belong!

And Bruj was talking his place!

5

Preparations

"Grass for the herds, herds for the people, people for the tribes," Gath hummed the hunting song as he hafted short bone handles onto flat-flaked stones, tying them with thongs soaked in wet glue. He was making a new set of burins for the Gatherers.

The days were bright, with little snowfall. New grass turned the riverbanks pale green, the earliest plants put out shoots. Fires were banked down earlier as people enjoyed warmer weather.

Jigd and his mate Roni of River Hearth sunned and

laid out bed furs in the outer cave and cleaned water pouches. Even children helped to sweep out the rushes and the ticks that had made their home with them in the long Freeze.

Baskets made of dried grass, made in previous Growings were repaired—polished with melted fat to keep them supple. They would be taken down to the river to soak, repeating the process until they were good as new.

There was noise and talk.

Hunters arrived from other tribes. At Carver's Hearth toolmakers worked all day—sharpening blunted flints, replacing broken handles of axes and spears and repairing cooking tools. By evening a pile of waste bone shards were sorted by someone or other before being swept into hearth fires. Larger stone and bone flakes were put away, too precious to throw, while some found new uses as digging tools, small spoons and objects. Shiga worked but continued to sleep in the outer cave.

Urm loved to carve small ornaments and cooking utensils and usually Shiga saved her some good pieces. But this time Urm stayed away.

What had always been the busiest and happiest time

of the year for Shiga became days to be borne alone. Shiga seldom spoke to anyone at all, though he tried very hard to welcome the hunters coming.

Gath's sharp eyes were on everyone, checking, making sure tools were accurately made. But he kept Shiga especially busy often gazing at him with a worried frown.

Shiga worked hard. It kept his mind off the Hunt, of Urm and how mean he had been to her; it made him notice Bruj who thumped newcomers and laughed and spoke loudly about First Hunt. Bruj spent the evenings at Mother Hearth.

So Shiga avoided Mother Hearth; Bruj had replaced him—so there was no point—he was smiling and laughing with Tribe Mother and whoever happened to be there—and especially with Urm.

Occasionally, he noticed Urm's glances. He would have liked to apologise but she was never alone; her days were busy preparing and packing medicines. And her evenings seemed to be with Bruj! Besides he felt ashamed—while she was Hunt Maiden, he wasn't yet considered a hunter!

Sometimes it took all his will not to go up to them and drag Bruj away who behaved as if he belonged there!

One evening he saw Bruj helping Urm pack the little medicine pouches the hunters carried. Shiga focused on fitting a new shaft-head he had carefully shaped, into the wooden handle he had made through the long Freeze. A sudden cry from Urm made him look up— she had dropped something and Bruj had a comforting arm on her back!

Shiga gritted his teeth and jammed the shaft head hard. It broke. With an angry grunt, he flung it into the fire. Ignoring the puzzled glances from those around, Shiga strode out.

Hil, sitting by him gave a long look at his retreating figure then glanced at Mother Hearth before going back to her work.

Shiga went into the store to search for a suitable piece—he doubted he would get one as good. He did not notice the look Duni and Hil exchanged.

He sorted idly—hating himself, hating Bruj— the grasping, sly fellow that he was! What did the tribespeople see in him? Did Urm even *like* him? She talked to him often enough, even if she had called him *wolf-whelp* at Fat Gathering—it seemed such a long time ago! *And* he had been so rude to her, she wasn't speaking to him! It wasn't her fault she was chosen to be Hunt Maiden—whatever they did! They had grown up together, Tribe Mother had been as good as his mother too. Oh why had he failed that silly initiation! Even last year he'd run away from First Hunt. Why would Urm not prefer Bruj? At times he felt more annoyed with himself than Bruj.

He picked up a long bone shaft—it would have to serve. Did no one notice how little Bruj helped with the preparations? And so thoughts circled in his head till he felt crazy.

The days grew longer- some evenings the toolmakers worked out on the ledge. Shiga preferred to be out, it was easier to ignore Bruj in the open air. Others stopped by to watch—offering advice, making jokes, which made Gath mutter and frown and led to teasing and laughter.

At these moments Shiga almost forgot his troubles.

Under Gath's careful guidance, he had learnt not just to make tools but also the care that went in choosing and testing them before a hunt. Why a point must be heated just right before being sharpened; why handles needed to be checked so thoroughly for cracks.

"You must not take the animal spirit lightly. See the fine crack here- in the middle. If that snaps, and a bison has been struck but not brought down, the hunter has no time to move out of his way."

Shiga had not forgotten those long-ago words. What they did now could save lives later. In spite of himself, Shiga enjoyed this togetherness, this sharing of skills and strengths of the tribes. Like the sacred mammoths whose stories he had heard, and the wolves, who in spite of their fierceness looked after their own, tribespeople cared for each other.

When in the midst of the hunters, he now listened carefully when someone spoke of a past hunt, and did not dismiss it as an empty boast.

As long as he did not think of the coming First Hunt, as long as he ignored Bruj and didn't mind not speaking to Urm.

Only at night did the dream-bison rear its bloody

head or Urm's eyes reproach him.

* * *

Shiga began to rise very early. Every dawn, before the first light touched the overhang, Shiga went to the strip of riverbank below their Cliff to practice his spear throw. On the narrow bank a few trees grew and there was little space, but a few man-lengths downstream, it bent around Mammoth Cliff, widening into a small wood. Shiga liked the quiet place.

Though his aim was good, Shiga felt his throw needed more strength to pierce tough hide. And so ignoring the bloody images of his dreams, Shiga practised.

It was four suns since the Ceremony when Shiga came down earlier than usual. That night, he had not slept at all—the dream occurred every time he shut his eyes. So Shiga left his bed-furs and picking up his spear, went down just before dawn.

The sky lightened. Shiga turned right walking a little way into the woods. The trees here were taller, receiving both eastern and western sun, sucking moisture from the river and protected from the worst winds by the Cliff. In the shelter of a dwarf larch, grew the first crocus flowers—as white as the ice from which it had sprouted. He picked one to give Urm then threw it away.

Cliff's base was covered in long grass and flowers. Elsewhere, patches of snow had melted and hardened over in the night; it crunched beneath his steps. The trees had begun sending out shy leaves.

The healers would soon come here to search out early herbs. He pictured Urm in the morning sunlight and wondered if she would accept his apology.

The walk calmed him. But he felt too tired to practice.

Of a sudden he stopped short—just ahead were fresh paw marks, faint but there—with a frown Shiga knelt to examine and drew in a sharp breath—wolf marks! The hairs on his neck stood up. Slowly he looked around, sniffed—nothing. He looked up—the eastern sun wasn't yet strong but small animals scurried in the sparse shrubs; movements in the branches told him of birds; if there had been a wolf, it wasn't here now.

He scraped a little of the snow—the wolf had passed by sometime before dawn. A lone wolf? How had the

Scouters missed it—and so near Cave! Why was it near human dwelling when food was getting plentiful again? It was not in a pack—that much was certain. What then had made a wolf come this way? Shiga's mind teemed with questions.

He hefted his spear carefully—the trees provided little cover. A lone wolf that had been driven from its pack—or left —perhaps starving! He followed the paw marks—they went on to where the bank curved around the Cliff towards the Marsh, then went river-wards.

So the wolf had come to the Cliff base then turned and crossed the river. Shiga scanned the opposite bank—only a few short twisted alders –that was all. Maybe it was passing, it had smelt the humans and decided to go elsewhere.

Shiga took a deep breath—he had to be sure if it was staying nearby or just passing. With Melt giving way to Growing, many animals would follow the river in search of food; but animals avoided Mammoth Cliff— it had been a human dwelling for countless seasons!

Urm could have come upon the wolf! Or Duni!

Shiga shuddered. He would have to inform Manuk or Gath; but he didn't want to sound a false alarm—and be laughed at. Things were bad enough and he knew many thought he was a coward.

Sunlight lit up the budding foliage. A wind whooshed through the trees and Shiga looked at the grasses hugging the Cliff base. They swayed in the breeze and Shiga noticed a small hole in the rock wall. Again, he sniffed the air—nothing.

Careful, holding the spear poised, Shiga crept nearer. A faint smell—a bit stale; then a very soft sound. But a wind sprung up swishing the branches and he couldn't be sure.

The hole was at knee-height. Perhaps the wolf had just stayed the night. Keeping a safe distance he crouched to its side.

The breeze stopped as suddenly as it had started. The trees threw shadows over the river. In the silence Shiga thought he heard soft breathing and faint squeaks. He listened and it came again.

A litter!

A she-wolf with litter below their home! Shiga bit his lip. He must talk to Manuk—before anyone—before

Urm came upon it. If they had to kill the wolf what would happen to the pups? Shiga bit his lip harder.

What terrible luck before First Hunt! Killing babies—wolf or not angered the Goddess—everyone knew that! And orphaning them was as good as killing. Only a desperate she-wolf would birth her litter so near humans.

A sudden rustle behind made Shiga whirl around, his heart thudding, preparing to fight an angry she-wolf. It was Bruj spying from behind a tree trunk.

Recovering quickly, Shiga put a finger to his lips. Bruj had no spear. Shiga pointed to the hole at the Cliff base.

"Wolf-litter" he mouthed.

Bruj's eyes widened.

Signalling him to follow, Shiga thoughtfully retraced his steps.

The wolf—if it was anywhere within a mile or two, had definitely heard them—and of course smelt them long before. She would be wary now.

Bruj was looking over his shoulder. So he was afraid too, Shiga hid a satisfactory smile.

As soon as they were out of the woods Bruj burst out, "You did not have the guts to kill them!"

"Kill the pups! Don't they teach you anything? Don't be a fool. We must inform Manuk," then thoughtfully, "It's probably a new pair starting a brand new pack. Or a mother who has lost its mate! But why here, so close to humans?"

"I didn't have a spear or I would have waited for her."

"Speak low! Huh! You would have fought a she-wolf alone! Huh!" Shiga gave a scornful look. "Can you be quiet—for once?" he spoke slowly as if to a dim-witted child.

They glared at each other for a while.

Then Shiga turned away, too worried to argue. "Wonder how the Scouters missed the wolf tracks— and a she-wolf doesn't leave her pups till the passing of a moon. She is definitely alone and needs to hunt."

"So you won't do anything—you coward!"

Shiga lifted his spear. "Why you… you are like a hyena always trailing…! It's not for me to decide. I must tell Manuk."

"You are afraid! And your tribe is too wimpy—or else how can they allow you—"

Shiga gripped Bruj around the neck and brought up

his spear point to his neck.

Bruj's eyes widened, he started edging to the left; Shiga gave him a hard shove, willing himself to calm down. He walked quickly away. Then he took aim with his spear and threw hard. It landed with a thwack into the young alder ahead. He heard Bruj climbing up the boulder-steps.

"Urm prefers proper hunters," said a low voice above his head. Shiga gritted his teeth and went to retrieve his spear. Only when he had reached the alder and yanked it away, did he realize it was the furthest he had ever thrown—a good eight and a half man-lengths!

6

Lies

Shiga spent the day sitting on the ledge overhang—working on the new shaft and making sure no one went to the woods. Both Manuk and Gath had left early with the Scouters, now he had to wait till evening. He didn't want to scare the others or worry Tribe Mother.

He didn't see Bruj the rest of the day and didn't care to.

Dusk fell still the Scouters didn't return, sometimes they camped out. Shiga went in to work by firelight at Carver's Hearth. Bruj stood talking to Tribe Mother, she was smiling so it wasn't about the wolf. At least he hadn't told anyone about it, creating panic.

The sleepless nights of the past days and the unaccustomed heat on the overhang made Shiga's head buzz. Too tired to bother with dinner, he fell asleep.

Late that night Shiga awoke. All around were sleeping bodies of hunters from other tribes—many he didn't know well. He could see outlines of banked fires in the main Cave. An owl hooted softly somewhere on the cliff-top.

Had he imagined it—would a wolf build her lair so close to humans? How had no one else seen her —she must have come to birth at least ten suns ago. Surely he had heard and smelt right.

Perhaps he should check again—come dawn. He must be sure before he spoke—if there was a wolf or he had dreamed of it like he did of the bison.

Would they really cast him out if he missed First Hunt? No one seemed to count all the small game he trapped. Till he hunted big game, he would not be called a hunter. He remembered last year being in the forest beside Lake, hearing the shouts, the mooing, grunting and dying wails of First Hunt. And he had thrown up there on the tree roots; sometimes he hated himself! Why did the strange dream visit him?

He lay awake a long time, tossing, and decided he could not leave without talking to Urm.

When he awoke, the Cave was empty, the sun streaming in. Remembering the wolf-den, Shiga threw aside his covers and scrambled up—he had overslept. He peered into the inner cave—only Nes and Tribe Mother talking in low voices; he grabbed his spear and ran out. not noticing Tribe Mother stop speaking to look at him.

Gath sat outside his head bent. Shiga greeted him, "Where is Manuk?" then seeing Gath too intent on some work to reply, he leapt down the boulder-steps. He would check quickly, then speak to Gath or Manuk.

He jumped down and turned towards the wood— Bruj and two young men, who were not there last night, stood—spears ready. Shiga nodded politely at the newcomers, who looked at him curiously. He turned to see Bruj smirking. What was the fool upto now?

"Had a good sleep? Refreshed?"

Shiga tried not to be annoyed at Bruj's mocking. In front of the newcomers too—he searched his mind for their names.

"Where's Manuk?" If Bruj had already told Manuk about the wolf, why had they not woken him?

"We are on guard! No one is to go into the wood. There is a wolf!" Bruj was showing off again.

"I was the one who found her lair yesterday, remember?" Shiga tried to match his tone. Bruj was brewing some trick but he had no time for this now.

Bruj gave an exaggerated yawn and grinned gesturing at the men. "And they just arrived—from Horse Tribe." Shiga forced a smile at the two. They nodded but did not smile.

Something was wrong!

Shiga glared at Bruj, "When did Manuk return? What did you tell him?" Oh if only he hadn't overslept! Goddess Mother couldn't she be on his side for once.

"I *had* to let them know—couldn't really go to sleep like a child!" Bruj's smile took in the men by his side. One of the men looked towards Shiga with a sneer.

"Manuk's orders. We have been here since dawn. A

lone wolf never approaches a group." Bruj spoke with mock patience.

Shiga whirled around without another word. He wasn't going to get anything from Bruj. He ran up. He squatted in front of the older man.

"When did you return? Have you been to the wolf-den?" It was true then, he hadn't imagined it!

Gath kept his eyes on his work. Shiga waited, Gath was rarely angry with him, but what had he done? Why had no one woken him up and sent him down to guard?

"Gath, please!" with great difficulty Shiga kept his voice from trembling.

Gath fixed him with a long, hard stare. Then he looked down and continued to work. "Sometimes I think—you do not belong—you do not care about the tribe."

Shiga squatted down heavily and put his head between his hands. "How can you say that?" his voice sounded strangled. "Just because I overslept! I was tired, ... I waited long, when you and Manuk didn't return last evening.... Besides I wasn't sure if it was a wolf-den—it could be a mistake, just pictures in my head again." The tears threatened to spill into his voice. "I meant to go down at first light to be sure, a wolf so near human dwelling!"

"You refused to tell! You told Bruj not to! You put everyone in danger!"

Shiga's eyes flared, "I did not! Why that lying, that wolf-whelp… did Bruj say that? Why that worm in the furs!"

"Calling him names, does not help. Did you refuse to tell about the wolf and ask him to be silent? Do you realize …" Gath was rarely this angry but Shiga no longer cared.

Shiga interrupted, "I told you I wasn't sure. I went down yesterday morning to practice and saw the wolf marks. Then the den, it seemed to have litter inside! I stayed here on the ledge the whole sun—so no one would go that way. Then when you and Manuk did not return, I fell asleep. I meant to check this morning … to be sure…"

Shiga bent his head to hide the tears he could no longer stop.

Everyone laughed at him, hated him, including

Gath. He really should leave—now. There was no way they would accept him, he never had been of the Tribe, just an orphan they had pitied.

Shiga brushed at his eyes, picked up his spear and went in.

He started to pack his few tools and necessities in a bundle—he wasn't going to stay here for a breath-space more—no one trusted him—they had known him since a baby but believed Bruj. He tied a knot and hung the small bundle onto his spear. He wished he could meet Urm—once but he had no idea where she was—the tears flowed he could not stop them and was thankful no one was around.

As he stood up to leave, Duni came out and scolded. 'Wait here for me. You haven't eaten dinner nor breakfast. A fine way to prepare for First Hunt.' She went outside without asking him what he was doing.

Shiga hesitated. Maybe he would take one last look inside for Urm and Tribe Mother—did they too believe Bruj!

He didn't hear the muted conversation out on the overhang.

"Gath how long have you known the boys?"

"Who?"

"Who but Shiga—and Bruj."

There was a muttered answer.

Shiga gazed at Tribe Mother, her back was turned intent on some work; maybe she didn't wish to speak to him too. Fresh tears sprung and Shiga swiped angrily at them. Urm wasn't there, she was barely seen since becoming Hunt Maiden. Shiga turned away, collected the new spear and a cloak now too short for him. He was ready to leave. Maybe he would at least tell Duni, she was always kind and she had asked him to wait. Perhaps he would have a last meal before he left the Tribe which had been his home. Shiga realized he was so hungry—he felt faint.

But it was Gath who walked in and stood there looking at him just as he used to when Shiga was little. Shiga lowered his head willing back the tears which didn't care what a fool he made of himself. Goddess he was a weakling!

"I am sorry I failed. I am leaving," he said.

Gath fumbled in his pouch and brought out some

dried berries. He offered it to Shiga.

"Eat first."

Shiga stared bewildered. There was a hint of a smile—what was happening?

But he was so hungry he took the berries.

7

Coming of the Herd

It was two suns since the wolf-den incident.

Stiff from sitting hunched so long, Shiga stood up and stretched.

There had been no chance to speak to Urm and they would be leaving any day now –soon as the herd passed by. The Scouters were busy, excitement mounted. They were so crowded now with hunters coming in everyday, that it would be a relief to start the trek to Lake. Providing food to so many just after Freeze even with contributions from in-coming hunters was no easy task!

Sitting on the ledge all day—Manuk had instructed him to work there, he barely saw Urm; she seemed to keep to the inner cave.

Shiga's brows furrowed. Gath had informed wryly that the Hunt Maiden could not speak to those who were yet to hunt.

But at least Gath and Manuk had believed him. Shiga swung his limbs in the warm afternoon air.

Manuk had called him and together with Gath, the three had checked the wooded area and wolf–den. There was a litter!

Neither Manuk nor Gath had spoken to Bruj since and Shiga had not missed Bruj's scowls.

"If you hear or see anything—any sign of the wolf, get the others. And you are not to go to that wood alone but with Gath or Rit!" Manuk had fixed him with a stern look, then given Shiga one of his rare smiles. With a grim face, he'd nodded towards where Bruj stood guard below Cliff, "I have told him too."

Everyone now knew that Shiga had discovered the wolf lair and Bruj had lied about him. Rit, one of the young men who'd been on guard that day, helped him scout the wood every morning and afternoon. Of the Horse Tribe, he was a great scouter and Shiga and Rit had become friends. It felt good; if Rit knew anything about his failed initiation, he did not say it.

Working on the ledge, a part of all the comings and goings—and avoiding Bruj—Shiga was busy helping repair and make tools for any hunter who asked him. He had even taken it on himself to collect Duni's plants from the wood. Her smile of pleasure had more than thanked him. Everytime he went to Duni, he hoped Urm would be there but she wasn't. Shiga hid his disappointment.

Everyone had been warned but Shiga could see few believed that a wolf would lair so near to humans, there had been no sign of the animal since—though one morning Shiga and Rit had seen fresh tracks and some scat near the river. It was a clever wolf.

Bruj had been instructed to remain on guard from dawn to dusk. Shiga wondered at his malice and couldn't help feel a small triumph. It was not for them to punish Bruj, he belonged to another tribe, but trying to destroy peace was serious—and the matter could be brought up at the Meet after First Hunt. Being stuck below the Cliff in the increasing heat and the swarming gnats was bad enough.

One afternoon Shiga walked into Cave—Gath had relieved him at the ledge for his meal—to find Urm sitting at Carver's Hearth, idly poking holes in a bit of leather. Most people had gone down to the river or were hunting small game, eager to spend as much time outdoors as they could; Tribe Mother and Duni could be heard in the storehouse. Ulm looked up and smiled at him—the first time since the Lighting! Signalling him to follow, she hurried out of the cave.

He saw his meal waiting at the Healer's Hearth—Duni usually left it there; quickly grabbing some, he sauntered out wondering how to get past Gath; but Gath had gone down.

Shiga knew where Urm had gone—he hurriedly skirted the cave-side along the narrow slope to the back, where the hillside slanted down like a mammoth's head giving Cliff its name.

Urm was waiting her legs dangling over the edge, onto the next slope, staring around. The bushes growing profusely prevented anyone from being seen easily. It was a secret place they had often used as children!

Urm nodded. "I am not to speak…"

Shiga sat down at a little distance suddenly tongue-tied.

The hill had shed its winter snow-coat. Campions, yellow poppies grew around and some ambitious marsh lavender brightened the hollows on the moist lower slopes of the Cliff.

A little barricade of bones ringed the narrow path to prevent accidental falls. But beyond that a steep path meandered down. It was seldom used.

"I am sorry, I was terribly rude." Shiga stared at a bush.

Urm had had time to think about the incident, she no longer felt as hurt but she was glad Shiga had apologized. She was beginning to think it was her imagination that their childhood togetherness had blossomed into something more.

After a while, she asked, 'You will be all right this time?'

Shiga saw the concern in her lovely eyes. Would he be?

He looked away, his feelings rushing through him, fear of the dream, apprehension of First Hunt, anger at Bruj and a fierce need to hold Urm tight and keep her safe. Overwhelmed, he looked around at the beauty of the land. His eyes prickled.

"It's the most beautiful home one could have. I will not let the Tribe down."

He didn't feel quite sure of himself—but he would try—by the Goddess he would. For Urm and Gath and Tribe Mother—for all this!

Shiga felt better, now that he'd spoken to Urm—it would have been awful to leave without a goodbye or a luck-wish. Gath and Manuk trusted him. Duni was kind. And he had a new friend—Rit of Horse Tribe. But most of all, Urm cared!

"Do you think we'll ever see the mammoths. Elder says when one walked by, the ground shook for many man-lengths around." Urm broke his reverie.

"Last year Tribe of Far Hill had seen one."

"I would love to see a mammoth."

"I would too. But we will only hunt it down."

"No we are not that bad!" she laid her hand on his arm. Shiga sat wishing this moment would never end.

"Mother says the tribes did not hunt them all the time—one mammoth could feed a tribe through Freeze. People only collected their bones from dying places. Do you know mammoths go to a special place when they grow old—to die? They say Mother Goddess calls to them."

"Perhaps that is why they are sacred." Shiga searched Urm's face. Why were they talking of elusive mammoths?

"Some say Mother Goddess is angry—we have hunted too many, so she's sent these bitter Freezes!"

Shiga laughed. "Elder or Gatherer's gossip?"

"I think they didn't have enough to eat… Elder tells of warmer days," said Urm.

Elder often told stories of when it had not been so cold. Shiga and Urm found that strange—the Freeze was always fierce, it brought starvation and illnesses— like it had taken his parents, whom he couldn't remember.

"If more animals go south, we will have to travel too. But Manuk says the mammoths are going far north-east-beyond Lake, to the end of the land. Just as well or we would have eaten them all."

Urm started to laugh.

"Shhh, we are not supposed to talk, remember," he reminded.

Urm shrugged. then asked, "Is there really a wolf in the wood?"

"Yes, I have seen the litter. Make sure you don't go there till it's killed."

"Poor mother wolf! Wonder why she was thrown out of the pack." It reminded her of the rule of being cast-out. She would not let it happen to Shiga!

Shiga was quiet. The lone wolf was a little like him! Except she had already been cast out. He wondered what she had done.

Shiga got up and stretched his arms as if to embrace the vast land.

"I want my Spirit to live here," he said.

"Duni is looking for you Urm." Tami came around the corner and hissed in a loud whisper, then gave Shiga a mischievous wink.

"Take good care Shiga," and with that she hurried away.

*   *   *

Late next morning, Zud the young Scouter returned panting. "Herd is sighted" he yelled, panting and gesturing to the east. "They're nearing Mammoth Cliff." Everyone came out to the ledge.

"How far?" Manuk pushed forward.

Someone gave Zud a pouch of water and he drank thirstily, spilling, waving his hands about, proud to have delivered the important message of the season. Manuk stood in front of him with legs planted apart and hands folded—impatient and frowning. Somehow he seemed larger before the Hunt, thought Shiga standing beside Gath.

"Apt name," said Gath under his breath.

"Zud-the ice storm" muttered Shiga. Hearing giggles he turned round to see Urm and Tami close by. Gath pretended not to hear.

"Half a day's run." Zud was pointing, upstream, "On their way to Lake. Came down yesterday... to the river… drink."

Shiga couldn't help smiling at his excitement. Manuk shaded his eyes and peered eastwards. The ice was blinding white in places it had not yet melted—though the dark patches of melting ice grew larger and the riverbank was a strip of green. He turned to Jigd.

"Light the ledge fires tonight. The tribes across need to hurry."

He would sound the first drum beat himself, to announce that it was time for First Hunt. Hunters who hadn't come to Mammoth Cliff, would make their way toward Lake.

Shiga felt a shiver run down his spine. It was time.

"It is ten suns since Fat Gathering, we start at dawn of the third sun from today." Manuk spoke with the authority of a Chief Huntsman.

People broke into murmured conversations—if they were busy before, it would be hectic now.

Zud who was having another drink interrupted. "Why not tomorrow, we could start tomorrow."

There were sniggers of laughter and Gath groaned.

Manuk fixed him with a glare. "You plan to lead the Hunt? Or be trampled by the herd?"

Young Zud lowered his head, chastened. Shiga

rolled his eyes—no one said much just before a hunt to Manuk, unless it was very important! But all the same he felt sorry for Zud.

Manuk was speaking again.

"We need to be well-prepared. And some from Far Hill need time to get here. Patience—without that there *can* be no hunt." His eyes surveyed the younger hunters—it rested on Shiga for a breath-space and then he turned to Gath.

Shiga felt his heartbeat speed up, Manuk may have trusted him about the wolf but he wasn't sure of him— Shiga wasn't sure of himself! He had vowed to the Goddess Mother and promised Urm—he would hunt this time. He noticed Bruj standing on the topmost boulder-step.

"The herd will likely pass this way tomorrow. Or the day after. Finish all outside chores today. No one must leave the Cave after that, not till the herd has passed. And no more bathing in the river till we hunters have left." Manuk looked pointedly at Urm.

Urm shifted her feet and Shiga stared at the water-bowl his ears turning pink. How did he know?

The other tribe huntsmen would time themselves

carefully, following after the herd at a safe distance. A sudden approach could scatter the herd or worse trigger a stampede and destroy months of work. The ledge fire was the signal that the herd was nearing Lake.

Shiga decided to speak to Rit—they must keep a close eye on Bruj—he was a trouble-maker, if there was one.

Manuk laid a hand on Zud's shoulder, muttered something to Nes and strode down the boulder-steps with Zud proudly following him.

Almost everyone had gone down to the river.

Gath still stood on the ledge his eyes far away. Shiga settled down to finish the little bowl he was carving for Tribe Mother. It was to be his gift before he left for First Hunt.

"What about the wolf?" Shiga asked his tone low.

"Meet us at moonrise. Tomorrow."

"Me?" Shiga stopped work to stare at Gath.

Gath just shrugged.

Shiga looked at the man who had been a father to

him always. Gath was trying so hard not to show his fears. Why was it so tough to do one thing for the people he loved? His throat tightened.

After a while gripping his spear Shiga ran down the boulders-steps.

No one stood guard! Had Bruj gone into the woods? Manuk had forbidden everyone; except when they went to check on the lair. Manuk would be displeased but everyone was busy. No animal would be around in all the noise that they had been making and so many spalshing at the river. Shiga walked carefully into the wood.

He walked slowly spear-ready, scanning for movement. The sun was high. Noises from Cave drifted down in snatches, Gath on the ledge was polishing something.

The sun went behind a passing cloud and the small wood took on a darker shade. The trees had grown their leaves fast to make most of the short summer. Shiga glanced at the river visible between the tree trunks—its waters thick and glittery. A fresh wind rose behind rustling the new leaves.

Shiga approached the bend, near the lair. No fresh tracks! He felt sorry for the she-wolf and her pups. Poor, desperate thing! They had found out she was scavenging in the midden, maybe she was hurt.

Soon she would be dead. But they didn't have a choice. All the same, Shiga felt guilty. He wondered if Manuk would agree to keep the pups till they were grown a bit—was it possible for humans to look after wolf pups?

Reaching the den, Shiga gasped. Three tiny wolf-pups lay outside the lair—their blood almost dry on their coats. Dead! Killed—their necks at odd angles. Shiga choked a sob, he bit his lip till the blood taste reached his tongue.

Bruj!

Shiga swallowed the rage and the vomit that rose into his mouth. No one—not one in the tribe of Healing Tree or any other would do this—it was forbidden to kill babies unless in self-defence. The bison-calf was the only time that they killed a young—and that too was a few years old.

Shiga backtracked. It was cruel and it was dangerous.

The mother-wolf if it came, would think it was him and rip him to pieces. How could she not smell this?

The fire would be lit tonight—and many would travel in twos and threes—an enraged wolf-mother who'd lost her babies would attack anyone.

Trying not to cry at the sight of those pathetic little bundles Shiga ran out of the woods. He would have liked to bury them but it was too risky.

Outside, he stood panting, scanning the plain for Manuk. The sounds of muttered conversations and laughter drifted down; no the mother wolf would not venture here till nightfall. Tribe Mother! They would have to tell her too.

It was Bruj—Shiga had no doubts! To kill two-week-old wolf pups and a wolf tribesman too! Shiga knew enough of the laws—Bruj would be in serious trouble once people knew!

Then he heard Manuk intently explaining something to Zud—he would have to get rid of Zud. One look at Shiga and Manuk quickened his pace. Shiga knew his face gave him away—he couldn't put away that sight.

Zud waved and Shiga waved back, smiling. Manuk said something to Zud, who nodded and ran past Shiga giving him a rough pat as he made for Tree.

"What is it, you look as if you have seen the spirits." The concern in his tone made Shiga's eyes fill—Manuk didn't think much of one who refused to hunt—and now Shiga couldn't even speak without turning tearful. He took a deep breath, then quickly told him.

Manuk's face turned as black as the snow clouds that gathered at the beginning of Freeze. He insisted on returning to the scene—with Shiga. "You were told not to come alone!"

Seeing the wolf-pups Manuk drew in a sharp breath.

"How do you know it was Bruj?"

"He was the only one who knew the lair. Apart from Rit and Lok."

"Such a beginning to First Hunt." Manuk looked at Shiga, his face troubled. "We have to kill the she-wolf. You know?"

Shiga nodded.

"Let's not mention this—to anyone, you understand? Go get Gath."

Shiga nodded again, he didn't trust himself to speak and went up.

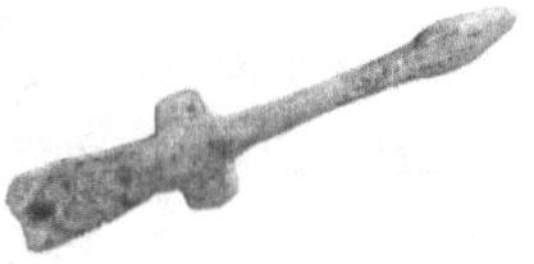

8

Creatures of the Goddess

The Cave was in chaos. Gath had not banked down his fire since the herd was sighted. Those who tried to sleep had a difficult time of it; there was a lot of grumbling from Elder.

Each huntsman carefully checked his spearheads and hafts. Older huntsmen patiently repeated instructions to eager youngsters.

"Hil, a few good points are better than a pouch heavy with spear-heads," Manuk told his daughter with a weary look.

"So eager. With a little care—" said Gath, after she left. He was fond of the strong and determined girl. Manuk grinned at his friend.

"Now you don't start, her mother is worried enough." He lowered his voice, "I have spoken to Jigd. Don't let Hil smell it though."

Gath smiled. "She will make a good hunt leader one day, once she has learnt patience." But his glance caught itself on Shiga, sitting with his head bent, sharpening something.

Manuk hurried out.

Bruj told to be at the Hunters' Hearth at all times, sullenly helped Nes. Shiga kept an eye to see if he was troubling her, she had far too much work.

Would Bruj be let off this heinous deed, wondered Shiga.

"We have to be sure it was him." Gath had said after the first shock and anger had worn off yesterday afternoon.

"Who else—"

Gath had laid an arm on his back,'This had better wait till the Meet.'

"It's wrong and it's unfair!" blurted Shiga.

"Nad is not going to like this—" Manuk ran his fingers through his hair and sighed heavily.

Urm and Tami were sorting dried plants. Urm had been to the back of Mammoth Cliff, to see if she could find some early cowberries. Shiga loved them. She had found them growing well on low ledges and had risked the steep path without anyone's knowledge.

When Tami saw her cleaning them, she had smiled, "I think I know who they are for."

Urm had pretended indifference, "You want some?"

"Oh no, not these, you will never forgive me if I eat these!" Tami laughed and Urm joined her.

"I risked my neck to get them," she whispered.

Shiga stretched and sauntered over to Mother Hearth.

"You two in charge of the common meal?" no one told him he could not talk to Tami.

"No. Roni and Nes will cook. We cook only soup—there are thirty people for today's evening meal," said Tami

Shiga rolled his eyes in mock relief and felt a tug on his hair.

"Since you have nothing to do, help us collect the fuel." Duni stood behind with her hands on her hips.

"Not before I get those cowberries," he pointed at the pile next to Urm. Duni laughed, but gave him a handful.

"Why me? The children can collect it," he grumbled.

All the same, he went around the five hearths. People fetched something from their own store pits—dried meat mostly and sometimes nuts. The River Hearth gave him a small bag of precious grass seeds, saved from what they had gathered last summer. That was generous indeed.

Shiga handed over the collected food.

Bruj's eyes followed him.

* * *

They had celebrated the news of the bison herd with Elder's special drink which he brewed all winter. Everyone had retired to their bed-fur, Manuk, Gath and Shiga had quietly slipped away.

Only Tribe Mother had seen them go—she had come out to the overhang and invoked whispered blessings on them—"Go with care." The signal fire on the ledge had burnt low and she fed it a little with dried twigs.

A thin scattering of frost made the boulder-steps, slippery.

Nearing the woods, Shiga stopped for a breath-space. The moonlight glittered on the river and threw sharp shadows on the water of the tree branches. Where he stood, lay in deep shadow—the firelight on the ledge invisible. The plains beyond the river shone in the moonlight.

Gath was sure the wolf hunted across the river away from their home—they crouched very near the boulder-steps. It was not safe to go further in the dark—there could be other animals hunting—it was Growing time after all.

"We'll see her alright—it's a waxing moon," whispered Manuk.

Shiga crouched in the now tall grass and heather. Bruised marsh lavender and thyme sent out a beautiful smell. Gath waited to his left, nearer the river. And Manuk squatted four man-lengths away to his right, watching the wood.

It had been agreed they would wait for Manuk's

signal before they did anything. And whoever saw the wolf first would tap his spear-butt.

Shiga looked all around—he had never been out at night except at Lake. Nights were dangerous. But it was also beautiful—white, pristine and silent—it seemed to wait for something.

An owl—probably the same he'd heard before spread out its snowy wings and whooshed away deeper into the wood. And that is when he saw the wolf.

Across the river—it stood still, waiting; it must have smelt them though the wind had shifted southeastwards over the last few days. But a wolf's smell and sight were very powerful. She must have smelt her dead cubs but dared not approach so many humans. Gath had buried them quietly and Tribe Mother had said prayers to Goddess Mother asking her to give them another life.

The she-wolf knew her life was in danger and yet …

Manuk's spear flew through the air just as she reached the water. She fell in with a splash and was soon carried away beyond the bend in the river. Manuk's spear went with it but it could not be helped.

Gath had said, wolves were wise, she had probably suspected something was wrong but what choice did she have. For a few breath-spaces Shiga saw her beautiful white coat darken with blood; maybe he could have prevented this.

When they returned Tribe Mother still sat on the ledge huddled in a bed-fur.

"Why are you here, it is too cold!" scolded Manuk. She gathered them around the ledge fire and spoke a few whispered words asking the Mother Goddess's forgiveness for what had happened.

Then she laid an arm on Shiga's head, 'You did a very brave thing.' Tribe Mother whispered.

He had wanted to hug her, bury his head in her arms; he had shaken his head in disagreement.

"We could have looked after the pups."

Gath laughed softly and ruffled his hair.

"I believe you would, my son."

Shiga was just glad of the darkness, he was crying too often nowadays.

* * *

Urm yawned and snuggled into her bed-furs. After the lively feast last night the hunters had left at dawn.

She had given the luck-wish to Shiga one last time. Oh Mother Goddess may he hunt this time and be safe—there were so many ways a hunter could meet his death.

She had managed to snatch one last moment with him; "Don't you want a drink?" she had asked, cautiously looking around to see if anyone noticed.

Looking up at her, Shiga had shaken his head.

She fed a long sliver of bone into the fire before them. It popped loudly. "You will be careful?"

"I am always careful, too careful," the bitterness touched Urm.

"Mother says care keeps us alive," the firelight left a sheen on his brown hair and nose.

They had smiled at each other.

In a way she was glad the hunters had left, it had become so noisy and crowded, she could barely think. And she had enough of some of the other tribespeople; especially nosy Bruj! There had been such ill-feeling between Shiga and Bruj—even Manuk seemed to have caught it.

Bruj had spent the last few days at Hunter's Hearth, he'd looked sullen but she noticed him following her with his eyes—she was glad they had all left!

Urm shrugged off the bedclothes.

The children still slept but others were busy about their tasks. Mostly women who did not hunt and Elder remained.

She prodded and shoved a few of the hot stones from the fire into a basket. Coming out on the ledge, she flung them into the water-bowl with a sizzle.

She washed and tilted her tingling face to the sky. The cold air made her gasp but she loved its feel on her skin.

It was a clear day—a right kind of day—to begin a First Hunt. The sun had already broken through the mist sending warm, searching fingers over the ledge. The air was crisp and quiet.

River White seemed friendlier. She could see a few people just where Shiga and she had been. She hugged the memory of that day of Fat Gathering.

Tree was growing her first green fur. Mother would be at healers' hut to pray for the success and safety of the hunters. She was glad to take her meal, there was much she wanted to ask.

Back inside, Urm put some dried meat on the hearthstones. While they warmed, she ground up some bulrush seeds and mixing with some water, prepared the flatbread Mother loved.

Leaving it to cook between two stones in the fire, she went over to Elder. He was rummaging amongst his belongings and muttering to himself. Roni at River hearth was sorting through her clothes trying to decide which ones could be washed and which ones had to be discarded. Cave was almost empty.

Urm sat next to Elder. "Would you like me to wash anything, Elder Father?"

"Huh?" Elder looked up startled, his rheumy eyes taking time to recognize Urm. He broke into a toothless smile. "You dear girl! Would you wash these for me?" He held up a pair of rhino wool trousers. Urm wrinkled her nose—they were probably as old as him and would have to be discarded.

"Let me do this for you," she started to sort through his stuff. Most of it was very dirty and she groaned inwardly—the first wash of the season was bad enough. Roni shot her a grateful look.

"I'll be back." Urm sighed and bundling Elder's washing went back to collect Mother's food.

As always after Melt, the walk to Tree was a great pleasure. She loitered, stopping at the green patches to see what was growing. Snow geese flew by overhead on their way to Lake where the fish would be plentiful.

She wondered about the bulrush seeds she had scattered in a moist spot a little away from where they usually grew, marking it with a small fence of bone. Would Shiga remember to check it? Would it really anger the Goddess if she grew Her plants? Bruj had helped to pick up the spilled bulrush seeds she carried in her pouch and asked her what she did with them. She had smiled as if it was just a whim but after that he had followed her activities even more; Urm had felt uncomfortable.

Tribe Mother had seen her and was coming down the ladder.

"Just in time, I'm ravenous."

They sat down below the growing canopy and munched their breakfast. Urm couldn't remember when she had Mother all to herself last.

There had been a little snowfall two nights ago and the place had been cleaned of all traces of the bison calf. The green of Tree shone and shimmered in the sunlight.

"Isn't it beautiful Mother?" Urm looked at the foliage above.

Her mother nodded and smiled.

"Did this too begin as a tiny plant?"

"Of course, but it lives much longer—no one remembers when she was a plant. Tree was here when our Tribespeople first came to this land. She is very old and few of her kind live except in the mountains. They say many such trees grew here before the mammoths came, before there were any people."

Urm wondered how Tree had got here so far from her own kind. Trees didn't move! "And our tribe named itself after Tree?"

"Tribe of Healing Tree. It is said one of our ancestors was a Healer. Tree was a sign from the Goddess to our tribe. She is just coming to fruit—soon you can smell them from even Marsh!" Mother laughed.

"Duni says they can make one remember, make one young," she found that a bit hard to believe.

Tribe Mother finished her breakfast.

"Do you think the seeds and roots we eat are alive? Like the ones I used for this bread?" Urm pointed to the last piece in her mother's hands.

Her mother held her gaze for a few heartbeats.

"They are, you know that. Till we cook them. That is why we ask the Goddess's permission to gather from her children."

"But does it hurt them to be plucked, like it hurts the bison and the foxes and antelopes?" the words tumbled out in a rush, bringing a memory of the Ceremony.

"I don't know Urm. Perhaps it does. But they are alive, that I know." Tribe Mother looked intently into her daughter's eyes. The thought of what Bruj had done bothered her and the fact that it had to be kept secret from everyone. And here was Urm with a different concern—one she didn't have the answer to.

"At last Gathering I have seen seeds attached to small plants. I pulled up a few …" Urm looked at her mother willing her to understand. "Of course I begged the Goddess's permission."

"And how do you know the Goddess gave it?" Shiga, Bruj and now Urm—all intent on challenging the timeless rules, Tribe Mother felt weary!

Urm stared into the distance, "You know how the same plants grow in the same place—most of the time."

"That is why it's easy to gather them. Just as the

bison move in herds, the plants remain in groups."

Urm turned towards her Mother. "Not always Mother. But most like to grow near water. And a seed has a baby plant within it—like a baby within a mother! So if I bury a seed in soil and give it water, it must grow. Even without its brethren. Like Tree." Urm finished in a rush. The words said aloud sounded strange.

Her mother did not answer for a very long time. Urm worried—maybe she was wrong—trying to change the ancient ways. Except, it didn't feel wrong!

"Yes, Tree." Tribe Mother said slowly looking at the ancient bole. Now why hadn't she thought of that. Tree grew all alone—how had she got here? Tribe Mother laid a hand on her daughter's head.

"I have spent years trying to understand the wishes of Goddess Mother. I do not have all the answers Urm. But food is not enough and the cold increases ... we still need hunters and gatherers." Mother fell silent.

"Do the old laws still apply?" Urm's heart gave a sudden lurch, she searched her mother's face thinking of Shiga.

"I do not make all the decisions Urm."

"Shiga has promised to see if anything is happening to the bulrush seeds I buried near Lake. If they grow there, we can grow them near here."

Her mother held up a hand. "The tribes will not believe so easily. And we must know if the Goddess approves. In everything.' She held her daughter's gaze for a few seconds then turned away but not before Urm saw the glisten in them.

"If there is any crisis—the tribes will blame you. And us. It will not be easy."

Urm wanted to ask about Shiga.

"Do not speak about it to anyone else. Take time to understand the secrets of the Goddess."

"Yes Mother," Urm didn't mention Bruj's curiosity about the spilled seeds. She hoped he would forget it all in the excitement of the Hunt!

"One other thing," her mother paused, "many will be interested to know if you have plans for Joining."

Urm's drew in her breath. "I am not ready!"

'There will young men at the Meet."

Urm gathered up her basket. The day had gone sour.

"Hunting is vital to our existence. No hunting—no food—no people!" Tribe Mother stood up and brushed down her skirt. "We will leave for Gathering in another twelve suns. And Urm before you go, wash the time-bones for me."

Urm nodded. And started to walk towards the river to join the others. Then she turned, "Mother there will be food—always!"

Her mother was half-way up to the Healer's Hut.

"I expect Shiga will grow up to be a wise man. In time," she looked resigned.

Urm could only nod. She felt like a snowflake—light and magical but just a touch of the sun could melt it.

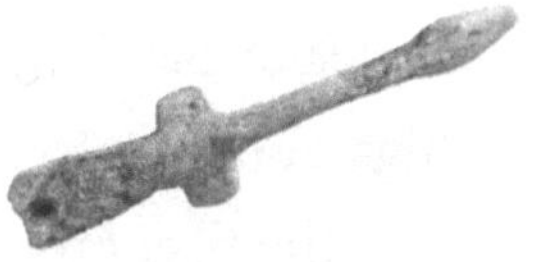

9

The Hunters

Just before nightfall the hunters reached Lake. Nad had led them at a fast trot for three suns; they had skirted the river by a quarter day's walk to prevent disturbing the bison herd. They had also stopped to repair the roofs of the huts at Rock Camp, which had been blown off in a Freeze blizzard.

Shiga and Rit threw down their loads gratefully.

A large fire was lit outside the huddle of huts, people of Lake having made things ready. They ate their first hot meal in three days—rabbits and small game hunted on the way, and some greens they had picked.

Lith—a senior Healer of Far Hill was given one of the smaller huts; Shiga and Rit stretched out near the door, a little way from the fire, preferring the open to the musty huts. One by one all the hunters settled, even the ones on guard dozed a bit.

Rit started to snore loudly drawing muttered grumblings. Shiga smiled; he was dreading First Hunt but the days trekking to Lake had passed pleasantly enough.

Rit and he had got along very well and he had even been drawn into conversations with other young hunters;

Bruj spent most of his time with the Wolf tribespeople and Shiga had not missed their furtive glances—he could not help wondering what he was up to now! Why could he not leave him alone, but had to shake his hatred like a lion cub with its meat.

Shiga was glad he had no watch to keep this night— Manuk had given him the task of the first watch at every camp. Shiga had been glad—it was a good way to show his fellowship. Nevertheless, he was very tired.

At dawn, Shiga rose stiff legged and cold. Rit still slept as did most others inside the huts. The wind was cold, the fire low—he fed it some dried sticks and thought of the warm Cave and of Urm.

Two men stood deep in conversation near Lake's edge, looking like shadows from the Otherworld in the pre-dawn mist. He could make out Manuk's broad squat figure, with his back to the water; the other was probably Nad standing a head taller than even Manuk and broader. First Hunts were mostly led by Nad.

Shiga decided to take the longer path to Lakeshore. Nad was so unlike Manuk—with a short temper and little patience—Shiga had never found any reason to be near Nad—he knew it was Nad who had talked of the old laws that cast out those who did not hunt!

This time too, he often found Nad's eyes watching him, it made him uneasy. He was sure Bruj hadn't told him about killing the wolf-pups. He wondered what Nad would do when he heard—Bruj had not just broken the rules of Goddess Mother but killed their totem!

This side of Lakeshore was a wide, sandy stretch. Large pieces of ice still floated on Lake, but the snow on the shores had melted. Across, to the south-west, he could see the larch woods, with the night frost still shimmering on the branches. Lake was so big—one could never see all of it together.

Shiga felt the softly rising wind, still chilly from its sweep down the Great Ice River in the north. The new sun rose behind the huts at his back, its thin rays not yet strong enough to reach inside the woods.

The eastern bank was already covered in young sedge and grasses but yet to reach full height. It was the best nesting ground for grouse and ptarmigan. Shiga's eye began to search out of habit for the best places to set his traps.

This year he was here to hunt bison, he reminded himself.

Shiga pulled off the stiff, sewn hide which covered three upturned canoes, he righted the light birch and skin crafts to inspect the damage of Freeze. One had a hole in it. The other two were usable—just a rubbing down with fat was all they needed. It could wait, now he wanted to see Lake—to be alone one last time.

People were already stirring and talking.

Taking the light paddle lying inside, he pushed the canoe into the frigid water. As he climbed in he saw Manuk standing alone, his eyebrows scrunched in thought.

He started to row. The canoe slid over the water, pushing away small ice floes. The land breeze continued; to his right in the northwest, was the river-break, where White meandered into Lake in numerous channels and little streams. Shiga gave it and its undercurrents a wide berth and rowed towards the woods.

About a hundred man-lengths from shore, he stopped. A ptarmigan flew out from the grasses, making towards the woods, in search of worms. Voices from the shore floated up.

Shiga rowed again, slowly, a little further, then let the canoe drift—it bobbed gently on the water.

Honks of snow geese told him of a gathering somewhere at the thin line of eastern shore. Twitterings and chirpings came from the nearest part of the little wood: blue robins would be starting to mate and blackbirds were singing. The sun grew stronger. Below him the waters rippled ever so gently as a large fish swam by—its dark shadow visible. If he speared it, it would make a tasty addition to their meals but somehow Shiga didn't want to destroy the lives pulsating in and over Lake just now. Soon enough, the killings would begin.

Lake was the next best place after Mammoth Cliff. The Growing here was humming—teeming with the children of the Goddess—in numbers he never saw anywhere else. As the sun warmed, dragon flies came out of the grasses, their iridescent wings glowing; a crane stood silently near the tall sedges at the river mouth, looking at him with annoyance—she would have to go further now if she wanted to fish in peace.

And much as he loved the white of snow—the green on Lake's shores was so restful—it almost allowed him to forget the great test he had to face.

"Don't look at the animal's eyes," Duni had whispered as he took her leave, "Just on the hunt, on your fellow hunters. When you look at the eyes, the animal spirit speaks to you."

"How do you know?" he had asked—had Duni ever hunted but he knew he only returned to his traps after the animal had died and he always avoided looking at their eyes.

Duni had smiled, then said seriously, "Don't let us down." Dear Duni.

With a deep breath, Shiga closed his eyes letting Lake's throbbing essence seep into him. "I won't," he whispered into the breeze.

A gentle rocking roused him. He looked around to see Rit rowing towards him. Sighing Shiga picked up the oars. The barricade at the edge of the eastern bog would have to be repaired before the Chasers left.

The two canoes bobbed next to each other. Rit's eyes looked troubled as he gazed at the peaceful beauty around him.

After a while, he turned to Shiga, "What happened to those wolf-pups?"

Shiga pursed his lips, "Why?" Manuk had said it wasn't to be mentioned.

"I want to know—from you."

Shiga searched his face. Rit could be trusted! So he told Rit what he had found that afternoon when the bison-herd had been sighted. And how the she-wolf was killed.

"Manuk said nothing was to be mentioned before First Hunt."

Rit gave a low whistle when he had finished. His normally twinkling eyes filled with the flash of anger—"That sly hyena! He has been telling the Wolf Tribe that you killed the wolf-pups!"

Shiga stood up almost overturning the canoe, Rit grabbed him down; both canoes bobbing furiously.

"Calm down Shiga, you will need all your wits."

Was that what Manuk and Nad were discussing this morning? Shiga could not think—he was angry and desperate.

They returned to shore. Pulling the canoes up the sand, Shiga went into the hut to fetch fat from their supplies—to rub them down. His morning's mood had gone but it would take the Goddesses' wrath to make him react, he decided. Rit was right. He needed to be calm, to think.

Out of the corner of his eyes he saw Bruj talking to Lith. Shiga didn't know what was happening anymore!

Killing the tribe totem was worse than not hunting. They would have to cast him out—and that wasn't old law! How would he prove it wasn't him but Bruj?

* * *

Shiga's canoe sailed along, a few paces away from the shore. Four young men apart from him, sat in it. It would be a few trips up and down to drop off all the menders.

The grassy ground between the bog and Lake was reached fastest by water. Otherwise it was half a day's walk around the shore. That was where they built the barricade for the big game.

None of the Wolf tribespeople had boarded his canoe. Shiga smarted under the insult—they weren't even giving him a chance to prove anything. He had to speak to Gath or Manuk, he had to know more.

They took it in turns to row. But Shiga refused any help, he continued to ferry the hunters for three trips till his arms felt they would drop off; it was the only way he could settle his churning mind.

Gath was already at the site with Nad. Manuk had stayed back with some others to mend the huts and the leaky canoe. As Shiga brought in the last four, he felt his arms could not even hold a hammerstone; he tied the canoe to a post stuck in the mud at the edge and jumped out.

"You are a strong rower—" someone looked up from his work of lashing two large bone pieces together. Shiga forced a smile. He rubbed his aching arms and looked around.

Nad was inspecting the old barricade for weak points. He scowled, "Don't stand around watching—get to work."

His face red, Shiga walked away quickly looking for a place where another pair of hands might be needed. He overheard mutters at the rudeness but no one would speak up to the Hunt Leader. Gath was nowhere to be seen, he would have to wait to speak to him.

"He's in a special bad mood!" whispered Guni of Lake, while other around gave him a curt nod. Shiga had joined them. Rit appeared next to him.

They were cutting down a bush. They never cut any

trees, if they could help it. Wood was precious. Old bones and horns left from earlier hunts provided a great many posts.

The work went fast. Out of the corner of his eye Shiga saw Bruj—maybe he should confront him here in front of everyone. He couldn't bear to wait till the Meet to clear his name. Why had Bruj killed the poor wolf-pups in the first place? Rit said he was jealous. Of what? Bruj was already a hunter. It was he—Shiga, who had to prove himself, not Bruj. Urm said—Shiga dropped the sharp-edged chopper almost on Rit's feet!

"Ow!!" Rit hopped rubbing his toe.

"Sorry! I wasn't careful …" Rit wasn't seriously hurt.

How had he not understood! All these moons he thought—what had he really thought? Just dealt with whatever happened! Bruj was doing everything he could—to prevent Shiga joining Urm!

Bruj had seen. "What do you expect? Hunt's around the corner!" he said to Rit. There was some laughter form the Wolf tribespeople.

Shiga rushed at him but Rit was quick. He held on to the tail of his tunic—"Shiga! Ignore him."

"I have ignored him long enough!"

One of the hunters from Wolf Tribe walked up to Bruj and dragged him away, giving Shiga a strange look.

The others had stopped to watch. It was a bit of excitement.

Gath strode up and laid an arm on Shiga's shoulder.

Breathing heavily, Shiga picked up the hammerstone. He could have hurt Rit badly—what was he thinking of? The gory bison-head came to mind. He winced.

Nad had walked up. "What's happening now?"

"Nothing" said Gath. Shiga and the others went back to work.

"There will be matters to discuss at the Meet," said Nad, his arms folded standing with legs apart.

"*Not before* First Hunt." Gath's voice had the hint of the hardest flint.

"All right, but we of the Wolf Tribe need answers."

By now everyone around had stopped their work—senior hunters squaring off was uncommon. Shiga's face flamed in embarrassment—everything that could go wrong was going wrong before First Hunt! A few of the Wolf tribe muttered and glared at him.

"And you will get them." Gath told Nad, then turned

on his heel and went back to his work.

There were a few sniggers and whispers. "Let's finish this," said Rit next to him.

Shiga wished he was far away from them all. If this was the tribes he was meant to hunt for—he was better off as a cast out!

That evening back at the huts Shiga sat by the fire outside, making a digging spade out of a hare's pelvis. It was to be a gift for Urm. A larger fire had been lit near the bigger huts and people were talking and singing. Rit had come to call him but Shiga had muttered an excuse, he needed to be alone. Gath had not spoken to him, nor Manuk.

A pair of large boots walked up and stopped on the opposite the fire. Nad. It would not do to ignore the Lead Hunter.

"The Chasers leave tomorrow. You will join them."

With a look of surprise Shiga stared. Chasers were the ablest and swiftest of the tribes.

He could only nod. It would be good to be roaming the land away from Bruj.

"All tribes will be represented—Bruj will be there

too. And I expect good behaviour from both of you. Come and see Mezad, he will be leading the Chasers."

Shiga's heart sank.

10

The Gatherers

The group walked downstream, following the riverbank opposite Mammoth Cliff. The children ran ahead, boisterous and noisy after being confined in Cave through Freeze. A few older men and women were helped along. Almost everyone carried gathering sacks and baskets. Two or three held spears, though it was unlikely they would be attacked—with the herds on the move the predators had enough to eat.

Everyone was relieved to be out in the open. In spite of the night-frost, pebbles and not snow crunched beneath their feet.

The foliage was dense along the river-bank; flowers dotted the growing grass. The children picked crocuses and lavender and ate the fresh petals. Spiderworts and ferns nodded alongside. Saxifrage had begun to peep over the wet ground, The women pointed things out to each other, noticing places of dense growth—these would be picked on their return in the late Growing.

Tami noticed a profusion of sphagnum moss and lichens on a boulder near the water's edge: she and Urm carefully went down the slippery bank. They sank to their heels in the mud but the long hide boots kept their feet from getting too wet. Pulling out blades from their belts, they scraped off the sphagnum in chunks— it was a great poultice for wounds. They flung it into their hide backpacks.

"There is a great variety of them—oh look," pleased, Tami pointed to the base of the boulder—tiny bracken ferns were growing. She cut them out, careful to leave a few to grow. It would be added to the evening soup.

Then noticed that Urm's mind was far away.

The Gatherers joked and laughed. Even Tribe Mother

joined in the fun. Near midday they left the riverbank and picked up a rhythmic jog along the stream which led to Rock Camp.

At the foothills of a rocky hillock to the south, was the Gatherers' Camp. Surrounded by low hills, it was green with growing things. Here large round huts stood, surrounded by a bone fence. A thin stream of water trickled down the rock-face behind. It was this they had followed upstream.

The Gatherers of Far Hill had already arrived. There were greetings and hugs and laughter.

Someone discovered a cache of early, mushrooms behind the huts. With the dry meats and the ferns this went into the large cooking baskets. Soon a most wonderful aroma of fresh stew spread through Rock Camp.

Tired from the long trek, most went to bed after dinner. A small fire burnt at the low doorway; it prevented large animals from making a home in the huts during Freeze.

A torch tied to the central pole smouldered but could be lit at a moment's notice. Two older women kept first watch, one near the door and the other by the pole, to prevent the torch from going out or the hut from catching fire.

Urm lay awake listening to the night sounds. She heard the chilling laughter of the hyenas, somewhere to the east. The hut felt so exposed, the night sounds so near. She was always happier in Cave. Urm pulled the furs a little more tightly over herself. Tami next to her was fast asleep.

She wondered how Shiga was getting along. It was so natural to wake up every morning, Freeze or Melt and see him.

The last few days she'd noticed Ina watching her often: what had Bruj told her about the seeds. Could they have possibly guessed what she was doing! Mother's warning took on a dreaded note. In the dark night Urm felt anxious. Sometimes all the pictures in her head got muddled.

She thought of Shiga's Initiation. It had been two very difficult years. Bruj had made matters worse with his sly ways; how could Mother think she would even consider Bruj! Oh Mother Goddess let Shiga take First Hunt seriously, she prayed.

She stared up at the newly made roof. She had never slept easily here even as a child. She remembered the warning stories of childhood—of how hyenas took away naughty babies. Instinctively, she looked to her right, where a figure of the Goddess Mother stood on a little stone block near the pole. Her mother and aunt slept on the earthen bench near it. The Goddess guarded the hut just as she guarded Cave when they were not there.

As she stared at the figure in the dark, it seemed to look back at her, as if telling her to rest. Slowly Urm's eyes closed. The hyenas had gone further away. She dreamt of masses of bulrushes growing below Mammoth Cliff—enough to feed them a whole Freeze; of Shiga leading the hunters across a frozen river—to a huge mammoth. But Shiga told everyone it was the last mammoth and so it was not to be hunted.

When she told Tami of her mammoth dream next morning, Tami said mammoth dreams were a good omen.

That day Gatherers of Wolf joined them. Ina was overjoyed to see them after a year; the next few days at Rock Camp were lively. They cleaned out the huts, repaired the earthen sleeping benches, put fresh earth on the dug-out floor. The last to come was Tribe of Horse and got an earful for taking their time. The Tribe of Lake gathered on its own.

Early every morning, the gatherers left in groups going in different directions, returning by late afternoon to the safety of the Camp. The old people stayed and minded the very young and sorted the stuff the groups brought back; they enjoyed the warm days and sometimes joined a group of gatherers if they felt like it. Many of them used slingshots to catch small game—hares and birds, sometimes a marmot or even a fox.

In the evening they prepared a hot meal—it had little meat but fragrant herbs and leaves and lots of nourishing roots growing on the hill sides. They sat around the fire outside the huts—talking, drumming and sometimes singing—songs of the Earth's kindness and beauty and ferocity, songs of gathering and joining. The summer evenings were long now and the sun stayed with them well past their evening meal.

They discussed what they had seen or collected, the

surprises and bounties the steppe lands always held. They told each other stories and ancient legends of magical plants which could heal and the skills and adventures of their mothers and grandmothers.

They talked of cures for ailments, cooking recipes and the dangers of child bearing and rearing.

The older women spent their time match-making. Normally Urm found it amusing, but not this year: every whisper and look in her direction made her think they were planning her joining to Bruj! What would happen if Shiga did not hunt this time? Shiga would keep his promise, she told herself.

Urm wished she could tell her aunt or at least Tami of her seeds but Mother's warning and Ina's shadowing stopped her.

But when they wandered about gathering, she carefully noted where each plant grew, how the place was different from others, whether it liked water or not and every detail she could think of. Each night she went over it all in her mind trying to memorise them.

One day on a whim, she decided to plant some seeds

near the stream behind Rock Camp. She dug tiny holes in the wet, rich mud and was just putting in seeds of oat grass, when Ina came to stand by her. In a panic, Urm quickly flung mud over them.

"What are you doing?" Ina narrowed her eyes looking very much like Bruj.

"Oh just—just checking—these seeds," flustered, Urm stood up dropping the rest.

Ina stared at the dropped oat seeds. "They don't grow here."

Urm brushed down her tunic, at a loss for words. "Found them uphill," she said and walked away, her heart thumping. She hoped Ina would forget the incident and not talk about it.

In the space of a few days, the land bore many flowers and fruits. Three suns before they left the Camp, Urm joined a group going the other side of Rock Hill. They were after everyone's favourite—the crowberries and cranberries. Rock Hill was known for its best berries.

Low creeping willows grew on its hillsides. Later they would boil its leaves and freeze them in ice. In the Freeze, when there were no fresh things, the tart leaves kept away illnesses of the skin and coughs and colds.

The stream had swelled with melt water and now ran swiftly downhill. Mosses and lichens covered the boulders over which it flowed and cow parsnips grew to its side. Elder made his foul-smelling drink—rak from it. She plucked some for Duni—for the sleep-bringing medicine.

Higher up the first shoots of asparagus peeped out of the grass. They walked on without touching them. The plants needed more days to grow.

Their days at Rock Camp were coming to an end. She wouldn't come here till next Growing. Who knows what would happen by then. Urm left the group and climbed to the top. As she stood catching her breath, she saw a lone bison running southwards across the plain. Three more half-grown bulls followed it. Urm realized these had been at the end of the herd and Goddess Mother had saved their lives. The hunt was on. Urm's heart fluttered within her.

The day before their journey was spent in storing, covering and tying the baskets and hide bags they had filled with the produce of the land. What they knew would spoil, they either ate, dried or pickled in last year's store of fat.

The rest would be left in the huts. On their return each tribe would take its share home. The crisp air would preserve it for many moons.

Normally Urm hated the gathering time to end but this year she was eager to reach Lake: to see how Shiga had fared, and the fate of her bulrush seeds. So much of her future depended on both.

11

The Chasers

Halfway down to Lake, River White forked , then nearing its western shores broke into many streams. Now torrents of melt water rushed into Lake—the ground hollowed by falling waters of many years—forming a churning rapid.

One after another two canoes slid past keeping a safe distance. Three people sat in each. Mezad and Lup, with Hil in one, Wyna, Shiga and Bruj in the other. Wyna, of the Tribe of Lake was their guide for she knew the Lakeshores with her eyes closed and Mezad of Horse Tribe was an experienced chaser. Shiga had taken Rit's place—it wasn't fair of Nad to do this. He wanted to be anywhere but with Bruj! It took all Shiga's willpower not to catch Bruj by the throat.

Once past the rapid, the canoes glided to the muddy shore near the woods.

Last night Shiga hadn't got a chance to speak to Manuk or Gath. Senior hunters had huddled together planning and he knew better than to disturb. But Rit had whispered to him that the Horse and other tribes were annoyed with Nad for his high-handedness.

"For a while there's been talk—the hunters feel he takes most decisions without consulting them. Then this…" Rit spread his hand to signify the incident at the barricade, "There will be talk and demand for proofs, they say; don't worry. And I am ok to give chasing a miss, I have things to do." Rit gave a mysterious smile.

With that Shiga had to be satisfied.

The group picked their way northwestwards and upstream, stepping across rivulets. Wyna led. Small larches sprang from the slippery, wet ground bending this way and that, as if they had drunk rak; crabs and large insects scurried out of their way. it was slippery with moss and green slime.

And Shiga forgot his troubles to focus on keeping his balance, up to his calves in mud. Bruj came last, stepping carefully, with Lup also from the Wolf Tribe slowing his pace to accompany him.

"Come on Bruj—chasers cannot be that slow." Hil teased, Bruj only scowled. Hil knew nothing of yesterday's incident.

Wyna pointed out mushrooms growing sheltered by the trees—in all colours and sizes and they picked a few edible ones.

Past the river-break the streams grew fewer, the ground still wet but firmer. Smaller boulders and pebbles had been swept into little piles on their mini shores. The going was easier.

The bison herd was further upstream on the opposite, eastern bank; without the chasers, they would move slowly, reaching Lake only at the mating time—in about fifteen suns. By then the female herd would have arrived too.

They had to steer them downstream, careful not to start a stampede, so that the male-herd arrived at Lake in a day or two; bison could travel fast when harried.

First Hunt needed to be over before the female herd arrived; they rarely killed cows, without them the herds would not multiply—as it is the Freeze took many. Though they managed, the tribe elders knew big game—and food was getting scarce.

They had been travelling at a smart trot for hours following the northern channel, when they came to the river-fork. They stopped for a brief rest refilling the water pouches. Wyna handed around dried meat and berries.

Shiga sat alone, nibbling at his food when Wyna offered a mushroom and squatted beside him; laughing as he grimaced biting on its raw, earthy taste;

"I prefer them cooked." Shiga couldn't help laughing with the vivacious Wyna; she was so like Hil in many ways except that she knew the plants very well too.

Now she pointed to the little strip at the river-fork. A profusion of plants and herbs grew there. "I will come here after the Hunt."

He nodded, if and after it was over, maybe he would bring Urm here one day….

"You interested in healing ?" asked Wyna.

Shiga stood up quickly, brushing the crumbs from

his clothes.

Mezad was inspecting the area carefully. "Once we can get the herd till here, we let them follow the other stream. Then we cross over to harry them."

He had taken over the lead.

* * *

As the sun descended towards the distant hills its rays hit them straight on, making them squint. They jogged steadily if a little slowly.

Shiga was exhausted travelling since dawn and trying to think of a way to clear his name—his head throbbed, the backpack felt heavier than in the morning. Though Bruj had remained quiet, Lup gave him angry glances. Shiga thought back to that day he'd come across the wolf-pups. Manuk should have spoken to the tribe, it might have saved him! How was he to prove Bruj had killed the pups. And so he did not notice the herd till Hil suddenly dropped on her haunches with Wyna following; quickly, everyone dropped to the ground. The herd grazed across the river some hundred man-lengths away.

Shiga counted—there were less than thirty bison!

Such a small herd. They needed to hunt at least fifteen or twenty to feed the tribes through Freeze—it would dwindle the numbers drastically! Goddess knew what would happen the coming year! He forgot his troubles.

The Chasers crept forward, keeping behind a rise in the bank—till they came to the huge bull—the leader; its horns were over a man's length wide. Its mane was black unlike the reddish brown fur of others and guard-hairs hung down past its knees. A magnificent animal!

Every once in a while the bull raised its enormous head to sniff the air—trying to smell the female herd which would soon come down to Lake; he was also checking for danger.

Shiga stayed at the back and tried not to look at the bull.

They crept away from the river stopping at a high knoll, which hid them from view. "Let's shelter there." Wyna pointed to a solitary rock next to a larch, forty man-lengths away.

Mezad nodded. "Speak low. I am going to scout."

"I will come with you," offered Bruj.

"Not now," with a brief smile, Mezad left. It did not improve Bruj's mood!

Arriving at the larch, Wyna took charge.

"Bruj—Shiga get firewood."

Shiga sighed inwardly. It was as if the Goddess Herself was throwing them together; short of sounding rude, he couldn't refuse, or tell Wyna that he no longer trusted himself not to fight Bruj. He felt Hil and Lup's gaze on him and ignoring it, turned to survey the riverbank. They needed to go far upstream or down to avoid alerting the herd; Shiga decided he would go upstream but first he made for some bushes at the base of the knoll. He had better get used to this, he needed to stop imagining gory bull heads if he was going to face First Hunt.

The bull had wandered to a place right across the knoll. Hiding in the grass, Shiga forced himself to look at its massive bulk across the waters. It was two man-lengths high at its shoulders, with an immense head. 'Mother Goddess!' Shiga breathed her name for strength.

His heart beat fast and his temples throbbed.

Squatting on his haunches, Shiga looked around—no Bruj! He pushed away the image of the bloody head and breathed deeply as Duni had taught him to.

After a while he felt better. He moved carefully away from the river, upstream, then at a safe distance stood up; the land here was undulating, in another half a day's jog northeastwards, it would give way to the flatter marshlands. Shiga strolled collecting any driftwood and bones—there was always plenty of the latter after Freeze, when weaker and starving animals died; he would be all right he told himself. But he must stop thinking about it, stop seeing things in his head.

Tall grasses waved and Shiga noticed burrows—hares, plenty of them! Quickly, he set a simple trap with thongs and a forked piece of driftwood. He resolved to skin and prepare what he caught this time. Shiga walked back towards the shelter feeling a bit braver.

"Been setting your bird traps?" Bruj dumped a load of driftwood next to his. Taking out his flintstones, he attempted to light the sticks Shiga had just arranged.

"You are a liar and a killer of your totem! How could you?" Shiga spat forgetting to keep his voice low.

"No one saw me." Bruj smiled. A spark flew from the flints to the wood, setting a tiny flame. "Urm won't join you."

"Why you…" Shiga spluttered then stopped—Wyna stood staring quizzically from one to the other.

"I think we need more wood." Shiga marched away.

He heard Bruj laugh but Wyna did not join in.

When he returned, two large sewn furs were strung onto the lower branches of the larch and then over the rock. The loose edge was propped by two poles cut from branches of the Tree.

"Where did these come from?" they looked too big for the compact backpacks.

"It's my winter coat. I just shed it." Wyna laughed.

The fire was burning well and Wyna was heating stones for the cooking.

Shiga arranged the firewood and bones in a neat pile; that should see them through the night. He looked up—the sun had disappeared and the dark was drawing in.

"I will just check if my trap has caught anything."

"Be back quick. Lup and Hil have gone too." Wyna was chopping the cattails and the mushrooms they had collected. Bruj hovered around.

Shiga returned with a large hare hanging from his hands. He refused Mezad's help and skinned and gutted the hare behind the rock; no one saw him swallow the vomit that rose in his throat.

As they ate, Hil congratulated Shiga—she and Lup had returned empty-handed.

* * *

"Don't you sleep?" groaned Shiga sitting up, rubbing his eyes as Wyna shook him awake.

They sipped the wormwood tea Lup had made.

Mezad had gone to peer over the knoll. He returned looking pleased—"The herd's moving downstream," he gestured at their group, "we've disturbed them."

They broke camp quickly. The bones and trash were buried in a shallow pit. Apart from the charred ring and two broken branches they left no trace of their camp.

The Chasers retraced their way.

"The grass near the fork will hold them," said Mezad but they jogged along not wasting time.

As the herd came in sight, again they dropped to the ground behind the tall grasses.

"Come along,' Wyna whispered to Shiga, then inched ahead on all fours as near to the water as she could.

Shiga kept pace, Wyna slithered like a snake not minding that her tunic was ruined in the mud!

"The bull is very old," she whispered in his ear. "Wonder no other young male has taken over. Such a small herd too!"

"Cold got them."

"This bull's experience keeps them alive, they know."

The herd across the river grazed on, unsuspecting.

"Pity!" ventured Shiga. Wyna looked at him, surprised, then nodded.

"Wish there was other food," she was nice and cared, thought Shiga with some surprise.

"Now watch!" Wyna cupped her hands to her mouth and honked like a snow goose—thrice—"It's the signal to start the Chase."

"Scouters waiting beyond river-break will hear, then transfer the signal call to the hunters at Lake," Wyna whispered.

Soon enough Shiga heard a faint honking, but only because he had been listening closely.

The herd at the river fork huddled together as if sensing something. The bull looked up as if it had seen them across the river.

"Now!" Wyna nudged him and stood up. They all stood and began to walk slowly toward the water. When they reached the water's edge, the bull put its head down and snorted in a warning then ambled downriver. The herd followed, nervous at the sight of the humans.

They did not cross: just walked keeping the herd in sight, so the bison were forced to move ahead.

Both herd and human group neared the muddy grounds of river-break; the distance between them was larger as the Chasers slowed. The herd was now forced to move northwards in order to avoid the dangerous river-break. Soon even stragglers had moved away.

The chasers walked away from the riverbank. Wyna gave another three goose calls and was answered again.

"That bull thinks that was a good goose," Shiga

grinned. Wyna gave a playful knock on his head and Shiga ducked.

"Pray the Goddess Mother, the bison recovers from the Freeze." Mezad stared after the departing herd, a worried frown on his face.

"Only thirty!" Lup was shaking his head.

"They say it has never been so cold," answered Hil.

"I have seen bison herds of over hundreds. We have lost two children this Freeze."

Shiga noticed Mezad's hair had white strands even though he was so strong and muscled; he looked resigned and sad.

They bent their heads in quiet sympathy.

After a brief rest, they crossed the river—swimming in the central deep part—and set up camp on the other side. Wet clothes were hung out to dry. Gathering fuel was easier, as this side of the river was greener and soon a stew bubbled on the fire—with the remains of the hare and mushrooms and ferns. Shiga felt a glow inside him which was not from the fire.

* * *

The fire was burning low; Shiga sitting in the opening

wished he was inside the make-shift shelter where warm sleeping bodies would keep his teeth from chattering. He threw a few sticks into the fire, his fingers ached. He had the last watch, soon it would be morning. His head began to droop.

Something startled him. Immediately alert, Shiga reached for his spear. He peered into the darkness. Shiga's blood froze!

A pair of burning embers floated just three man-lengths away. Two, three, four pairs. His neck hairs rose. Shiga's spear hand readied itself. Slowly he turned his head around. More pairs of the yellow burning embers were scattered in the middle distance.

Hyenas! A whole pack!

Ever so slowly, Shiga reached for a long branch at his side; he shifted it slightly till its other end lay in the fire. It caught and he stood up with it, "Scat! Go."

The hyenas retreated—just a little.

Mezad and Lup burst out of the shelter—spears at the ready. Lup took aim at the nearest and threw. There was a yelp. It had hit its mark but not fatally. The hyenas melted away in the darkness. Wyna and Hil were out too, they were feeding the fire higher till it blazed to half-man height. Retreating a little from the blazing heat they sat around it. Shiga noticed that Bruj sat almost inside the shelter. He smiled—Bruj was afraid!

Mezad looked towards the eastern sky. "Dawn isn't too far. I will keep watch with you."

"They are following the herd." Lup's face was grim. This complicated their work.

"We must start at first light—or they may scatter the herd—"

They did not voice that once the hyenas gave chase, there was little chance of getting the herd to the barricade. It would mean no First Hunt!

"You will need your strength, go back to sleep." said Mezad. Everyone gladly went inside the makeshift tent. Except Shiga. "I will watch your back."

The fire blazed. Once in a while Shiga and Mezad circled the shelter from the two ends meeting at the back and circling back to the fire. There was no large rock at their back this night.

"What's with you and Bruj?" asked Mezad after a

while. So he had not heard about the wolf-pups.

Shiga's ears burned with embarrassment, it sounded like a children's quarrel. Yet the injustice of the blame and the worry of clearing his name had nothing childish about it.

The absolute darkness around, the shared danger and the cozy fire made Shiga tell Mezad everything that had happened since he had seen the wolf marks below Mammoth Cliff—how Bruj followed him to the wolf-den below their Cliff and how he had told Manuk and Tribe Mother that Shiga had refused to warn them; and how when Shiga was thinking of a way to save the wolf-pups he had found them killed.

"And now he has told the Wolf Tribe I have killed the wolf-pups!" Shiga finished with bitterness.

Mezad was silent. But Shiga felt a strange relief.

Hil had come out of the shelter and sitting close to Shiga, shared her fur blanket with him. Shiga didn't mind her listening, she probably knew it all.

"Are you sure it was him?" asked Mezad. His eyes looked troubled. "It's his Tribe totem!"

"Only he knew! But I have no way to prove" Shiga's voice carried the frustration and bitterness of the past days. "And he will probably be believed, not someone who has yet to—"

Hil put an arm around him. "I heard Mother and Father discussing the wolf-pups in whispers. They thought I was asleep but something had woken me. The next morning—the day we sighted the herd I went down early and wondered if I could find the she-wolf."

Seeing their looks she added hastily, "Foolish I know, but I did it," after a while she said, "That is when I saw Bruj come out of the woods below our Cliff. He was surprised to see me but laughed and insisted I show him a specific kind of throw. So I didn't get to the woods; that day the herd was sighted and we got so busy what with the excitement of Hunt and arriving guests, I forgot; then Father said a she-wolf was killed. I didn't know the pups had been killed or I would have probably remembered…"

A sigh left Shiga's lungs and he lay down next to the fire. He felt very tired.

The sky was a pink wash. The fire had burnt low when Shiga awoke from his nap. Soon breakfast was done—Hil had found a large patch of berries in the shade of a dwarf alder and they had had their fill washed down with fresh river water. Like the camp before, within minutes they had cleared up and were ready to leave.

As they trotted downstream, Lup joined Shiga. After some polite talk, suddenly Lup touched his arm gently, "I am sorry—it should not have happened."

Surprised Shiga could only nod, then asked, "What will the Wolf Tribe do?"

"I don't know, but Nad must know the truth. I wonder why Manuk didn't tell him."

"Avoiding tension before the Hunt?" said Shiga. His sense of relief was so overwhelming, his legs felt weak: he slowed.

Hil joined them and winded her arms with Lup.

That was why Lup had a change of heart! Hil had told him. They were going to Join! Shiga grinned.

It also made him miss Urm.

They came upon traces of the hyenas following in the path of the herd which seemed to have gone faster; soon they caught up with the hyenas—who didn't seem to be in any hurry. They began to shout and scream, throwing stones and whatever they could find.

It was daytime, they were in a group and unlikely to be attacked. The hyenas ran off upstream, abandoning the herd's tracks and Shiga stared after them with loathing.

Mezad too was staring but further at the specks in the distance.

"The female herd?" Mezad had shaded his eyes to look.

"So early!"

"We must hurry. First Hunt needs to be over before they get to Lake."

"The hyenas will find them easier game. That gives us time."

How many bison would be left after First Hunt? How many bison cows would the hyenas bring down? Sometimes he just could not understand the ways of the Goddess Mother!

12

First Hunt

It had taken longer than a day to harry the herd towards the eastern ground by the bog. But the Chasers knew rushing could create a stampede. Slowly, relentlessly, they had edged the herd towards Lake. The smell of tender grass and new plants made the work easier. Yet they hesitated, because they also smelt the humans. The hyenas had scared them already and they were not as calm as yesterday.

But it was after Freeze and they were hungry. Once the bull went, most of the herd had followed.

Inside, some twenty bison now cropped the grass,

occasionally looking at the barricade, as if trying to place it in their plodding minds. The Lake surrounded them in the south and west—to their east was the bog. It was peaceful except for the few humans who hovered around the barricade.

It was mid-morning. The bison had spent an evening and a night in the place, the wide gate in the northwest spanning the herd-path had been closed; the remaining herd outside the barricades had hesitated without their leader, then moved back upstream—nervous.

Outside the barricade now stood the hunters—almost shoulder to shoulder. Then the signal was given by Nad.

As huntsmen threw their spears, there was chaos. the bison had moved as far from the barricade as they could—to the edge of Lake; they did not stop munching the sweet grass—only looking up as the spears came down on them. For most it was their last look. A few young bulls charged the barricade but it held—it was strongly built.

Shiga stood with the hunters—he tried not to see the suffering of the speared animals though their calls of agony rose above the voices of the hunters. He ignored the churnings in his stomach, focusing on a young bull. Good enough for his First Hunt—he threw his spear—the bull faced away, exposing its hind and side. The spear pierced its hamstrings. The young bull gave a fearful grunt and collapsed on its haunches. Shiga found himself sweating—his own calf muscles felt taut as he breathed heavily through his mouth and took careful aim a second time. He must not prolong the poor animal's agony.

The second spear on its neck had it fall on its side, its eyes rolling in terror. "Don't look at its eyes!" but Shiga saw them glazing over, the spirit leaving them; what happened to animal spirits in the Otherworld?

The bull he'd killed had probably seen only two Growings; at least it had eaten its fill!

"Well done" Shiga turned to see Rit. Shiga smiled his thanks and wished he could leave the place.

Mezad and Guni were bringing down another. An old bull lay on its side and Shiga tried to shut away its death call, as it lay bleeding from the neck. It had only one spear wound but the correct one. Most of the youngest bulls were dead already. It smelt of blood, terror and the blood-lust; dying bulls and hunters' cries stirred the air; Shiga tried not to throw up.

Four senior huntsmen stood close to his left; they had the lead bull covered. It was snorting a warning, preparing to charge . And it had the strength to break through. Nad, Manuk, and the Chief Hunters of Horse and Lake took careful aim—they could not afford to miss their mark. In spite of his repulsion, Shiga admired their synchronization, their focus on the bull and awareness of each other; he watched.

One after another, in quick succession four spears soared towards the bull's legs. The bull veered towards the gate, perhaps expecting a way of escape. Two of the spears missed. Nad exclaimed, frustrated!

But the other two spears pierced the bull's thick hide—one on its right flank and the other on its foreleg. It bellowed and turned back; none of the blows had brought it down, only enraged it.

Shiga stepped back from the barricade instinctively as did others. He could see the red of the bull's eyes as it charged towards the group of hunters but stopped short of the barricade. Another set of spears soared through the air.

Other hunters prepared to help, spears at the ready. Shiga could not move his eyes from the lead bull —he was massive, the brown-black fur shaggy and matted by snow and mud. Its horns swung out of its head- it could kill instantly, horribly. Shiga bent to pick another spear quickly checking its point, when there was a commotion to his right.

Looking up, his blood froze. Bruj had climbed into the barricade at the gate end and was making for the bull, which hadn't yet noticed him. The men about to throw their spears had frozen. Inside, Bruj was approaching the bull with his spear. Gath appeared near the gate; Lup, was running along the barricade towards them.

"Come back, you fool. Walk backwards and we'll lift you out." Gath's voice was hoarse and low.

Bruj walked on, his eyes like one who had no mind! The huge bull turned to see a new threat. The animal bent its head, pawing the ground.

Shiga's heart thudded till the blood in his ears seemed to roar. The fool would be gored to death! He stood no chance.

All at once Shiga shouted and Rit with a quick glance at him took it up. The bull stopped, moved its huge head slowly to its right and back towards Bruj. But it was not to be distracted from its quarry; blood seeped from its flank.

Bruj raised his spear for a throw, then stopped as if frozen in a sudden hail. Only his eyes widened in terror, as if he had just realized where he was.

Shiga had moved quietly and now stood his chest touching the barricade, about five man-lengths to the right of Bruj. Rit was right behind. He shook his spear and yelled. The spear-point caught the rays of the sun and glinted. The bull stopped and looked towards him, blinking. Rit caught on and started to shake his spear and the barricade.

The bull looked from Bruj to them, the hunters forgotten. Its front legs were now shivering from the blood loss. It moved towards Shiga. Still strong enough to charge—its weight alone could break the barricade and crush him, thought Shiga.

He gave another blood curdling yell and rattled the barricade, willing the bull to move towards him. There were exclamations and shouts of shock. Not just one boy who seemed to have gone mad, now there were three. The hunt seemed to be going horribly wrong.

The bull changed direction.

"Shiga, stop that!" commanded Manuk's angry voice. Shiga didn't turn but kept his gaze on the bull.

"We have to distract it!" he said without turning his head to the senior hunters who now stood beside him.

"Step back, walk backwards, very slowly. Don't—throw—the—spear," he told Bruj in a loud monotone still looking at the bull. But Bruj had frozen completely.

Shiga gave another rattle to the barricade as if he meant to break it down and yelled again. The bull began to move towards him.

By now the other hunters had rushed to Shiga or Gath's side, who was still trying to get Bruj to back out. With his free hand, Shiga signalled everyone back as he aimed his spear. He was twenty man-lengths away—too far to make a fatal hit.

There would be only one chance. He had to hit the bull on the neck, just to the side of his bent head. Otherwise, the bull would break through. The bull charged.

"Move back!" ordered Shiga, he was being crowded. But people had scattered fast to get out of the bull's range. Only Manuk stood his ground; and Nad behind him. Shiga waited for two breaths. Ten man-lengths!

Another deep breath—eight man-lengths.

Shiga flung his spear recalling Bruj's insults, Nad's sneers, the dead wolf-pups—and Urm.

The short spear sailed slowly in an arc—over the barricade and into the enclosure. Then it seemed to pick up speed and landed—a spear handle protruded from the bull's neck. The animal folded its front legs and fell with a loud bellow of agony. Shiga screwed shut his eyes, his head reeled—the dream was coming true.

Within a few breath spaces, a barrage of spears was thrown. The lead bull now bristled with spears but the life spirit was too strong to be driven away so soon. It lay bleeding profusely amongst its dead herd members.

Its head rested on the ground, reddening the earth. Only its eyes seemed to look straight ahead—at Shiga. Accusingly!

"Forgive me," Shiga murmured, his hands on his bent knees, panting. He felt immensely sad and didn't bother to wipe the tears which flowed, "Goddess Mother forgive me." He tried to tell himself it was to be killed anyway.

Then he found himself on Mezad's shoulder. Lup was offering him a drink from a pouch! Manuk was slapping his back. The hunters of all tribes were gathered around cheering.

He noticed Bruj was now outside the barricade, Lith leading him away. He turned to stare at Shiga, once.

Shiga felt his anger disappear. It was going to be bad for Bruj—endangering First Hunt, challenging the bison-spirit, and killing the tribe totem! He did not want to be in Bruj's place facing the elders at the Meeting. The boy must be touched, how else could one do such foolish things! Did he really believe Urm would admire him? Shiga saw Nad, his face grim striding towards Bruj. The celebrating group moved toward the huts—Shiga forgot about Bruj, about his fears; it felt good to be carried with honour!

But he was aware that behind him within the barricade lay shaggy, bleeding mounds—the food for the tribe in the coming moons.

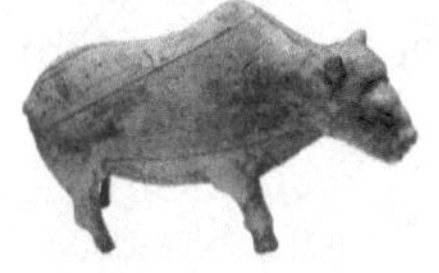

13

The Meet

The gatherers of the Tribe of Lake arrived the next morning. Everyone got busy skinning and cleaning the bison carcasses. The legs were cut off, then the animals were skinned . The thick skins with the fur were turned inside out and left to dry on the barricade fence. Then the meat and fat and innards were removed; carefully separating the intestine and the stomach. Some of it was cooked for their meals. Most of it was buried in the cold soil; the gatherers would arrive in a day or two and they would have enough people to complete the big work.

Gath never tired of hearing how Shiga had faced the bull and saved First Hunt. A funny pain filled Shiga's heart to see the older man's excitement. Manuk was all smiles and back-slaps.

One morning Gath and Shiga sat by the fire outside the huts at their usual task of sharpening and repairing broken tools. The hut was empty, most were at the kill-site.

Shiga decided to ask Gath about the dream.

Gath's was testing a spear-point carefully against the edge of his palm, "You could have come to me earlier son. I think I know what your dreams are about. It happened when you were only four Growings old."

Then he told Shiga. How a bull injured by a cave lion had turned rogue. It was in great pain and had taken to grazing near River White; how the hyenas or wolves had not got him was a wonder. His wound had festered and he would soon die. But in his enraged state he was dangerous.

Tribespeople feared to venture down from Mammoth Cliff. It had been, just after First Hunt. "You know how much work needs to be done after Growing—and we still needed to gather as long as the Growing lasted. So the Chief Huntsman took three skilled hunters with him to kill the bull." Gath paused for breath.

"Manuk?" said Shiga.

"Oh no, Manuk was a keen young hunter like Hil. It was another man, a brave man." Gath's eyes were full of the pain of remembering.

"The Chief Huntsman's spear struck the mad bull. But it charged and the other hunters missed. They scattered—except the Chief Huntsman. When he saw he could not outrun it, he attacked it with his axe. He killed the bull but it gored him badly. The hunters brought him back but he died. The healers did not even get a chance," there was a long pause.

"He was mate to Titha—our Tribe Mother—your Hearth Mother."

Shiga's eyes widened in shock. "Urm's father?" Gath nodded.

"We were on the ledge watching helplessly—trying to hold back Titha. No one noticed you had toddled out of Cave. You probably saw the whole thing.

We could not or did not go to his aid. Tribe Mother does not like to be reminded."

They sat in silence for a long time, an immense

feeling of loss welling up in both.

What a terrible thing thought Shiga but the dream, now explained had lost its power of terror.

Shiga cupped the tiny pouch of seeds in his palm— so light, so easily lost and yet so powerful, it could grow into a plant—into food. So Urm said and he believed her. Some way behind a growth of sedges, he hunkered down and made tiny holes in the soft ground, a few man-lengths from Lake. He dropped the seeds and covered them over. It seemed a strange thing to do, like preparing one for the Otherworld. Like they must have prepared his parents and Urm's father. He pushed the thought away, what use to think of it. Urm had asked him to do this. And he didn't care if anyone saw him. Making a tiny fence around the place, he returned to camp.

* * *

Two suns from the Hunt, all the Gatherers arrived in the afternoon laden with bulging baskets and hide bags. Nad had sent out some men to help them—Bruj amongst them. Shiga hadn't liked the thought of him meeting Urm first but when he had wanted to go, Gath had stopped him.

"Let be Shiga! Let him get away from angry men and mocking looks. It will not be easy for him at Meet."

Shiga had seen it; and the teasing by the youngest hunters when no one was around; Bruj was not included in any work. Occassionally their eyes met, but before Bruj's customary scowl, Shiga had seen the confusion and sadness in his eyes. Shiga had felt sorry.

Urm came looking fresh and beautiful from her days in the sun. She gave him a brilliant smile and disappeared into the women's hut. Here at Lake, the men and women lived in separate huts. Shiga waited impatiently for the evening meal when he would see her. Did she know that he was now a hunter?

The day seemed so long that Shiga set off for the second time to check his snares. The birds would add variety to their meals and some of the meat could be smoked and kept.

The men had already started to plan the Full Hunt —when the animals were plump and the Goddess prepared to sleep for Freeze. They too would need to prepare for Freeze. Now that the gatherers had arrived with their bounty, meals would be better. He was fed up with roast bison meat.

But best of all Urm was here. Perhaps he should ask her about Joining! Suddenly Shiga felt unsure—what if she refused. Pulling out a canoe, Shiga went to his snares. And freed the baby bird who had caught on one. She wasn't too badly injured and would heal.

As he rowed back, the smell of cooking wafted from the shore. A large hearth had been built outside the huts. Pulling up the canoe, his eyes searched for Urm amongst the crowd. He found her standing by herself looking towards the western Lakeshore. With a pang Shiga remembered the plants she'd wanted him to check. He walked up to her.

"How was the gathering?" he had never felt so awkward talking to her!

"You didn't check the plants," she accused.

"I buried the oat-grass seeds." She didn't seem to have missed him one bit. Had she heard how he'd killed the bull. And saved that awful Bruj.

She took him by the hand and led him toward river-break. He shivered though his hand was warm in her grasp.

After a while they came near the first of the streams. Urm veered away from Lake walking along the thin stream.

"There," in a small patch of ground just where the sedges thinned away, there was a little square of uniform green. It was about a man's length on each side. The plants were half his height—bulrushes. The feathery heads were a mix of orange-red and green.

Shiga stared in amazement. This would be so easy to gather! Enough for an evening meal for the tribe!

"They have survived. I covered the seeds in wet lake sand for them to keep warm in Freeze. Now look at them!" Urm was breathless with excitement—like a new mother with her first-born.

It was magic. Unbelievable. It took entire moons of searching and gathering to get the amount of grass-seeds they needed for Freeze. Often there was just enough for the babies and old people—sometimes Hunt-feasts. And now Urm had made them grow together, where she wanted. It was hard to believe his eyes! Perhaps it was one of Goddess Mother's play...

But if they could make bulrushes grow, they could make other plants grow too! At least Urm could. It meant more food!

"Can you do this with other plants too?" Shiga whispered. It wasn't right to speak of such magic loudly.

Urm puckered her brows, "I think so. Some of the medicines we use, they don't need seeds, they can grow from a green twig and few leaves. I found one growing on the Healers' Hut on Tree. Mother or Duni must have dropped it there. But they need to be warm and they need water and light."

Shiga nodded, not knowing what to make of this miracle.

"What will you do now?" he asked, fearfully. It was forbidden to tamper with the Goddess's work.

"I will watch them—they are young yet. Seeds will only ripen at the end of Growing," then she added, "Mother says it's not the right time to speak of it."

"But you must show her!"

Urm nodded.

Somehow what he had done at the hunt did not seem so great now. Most people hunted—it was a necessary skill. But no one could grow things like Goddess Mother.

She slipped her hands into his and Shiga felt a lump in his throat. His Urm was clever—best Healer and one who seemed to know the ways of Goddess Mother —even more than Tribe Mother!

"Shiga I have to congratulate you on your First Hunt," she turned to smile.

Shiga just shook his head.

"You say you don't like to hunt. But you braved a lead bull to save Bruj and perhaps all the hunters." There was laughter in her voice, "I think I will forgive you this time for forgetting the plants," and she gave him a hug.

Shiga held her tight—and wondered if this was true. They had spent their entire childhood together, but never had it occurred to him to hug her. Her hood was pushed back and her hair was the colour of the sun in the Late Growing—now all dishevelled. He bent his head and breathed deeply. It smelt of earth and air, of the warm Growing. His heart was light as a flying bird. Then he found the courage to ask.

"Have you thought about Joining?"

A deep sigh went through Urm and he felt her shiver. Then she looked up with a gleam in her eyes, "I will think about it. Joining a man with such an aim must be thought about carefully." She didn't add a man with the courage to think of others, a man who felt the spirits around him in animals and plants. Shiga gave her a squeeze and then bent his head over her face.

* * *

The Tribe elders had called Shiga in to the Meet; as Shiga entered, bowing his head to all the Tribe Mothers, Chief Healers and Hunters in the hut he caught Bruj sitting in a corner, with Ina by his side.

Bruj was staring at the floor—his hair was unkempt, when he looked up, his eyes were glazed. He reminded Shiga of the hunted bisons. Was this the same boy who had spent the year taunting him? He caught Ina's hateful glance and felt sorry; they looked so lost.

But Nad was asking him, "What do you know of the wolf pups?"

Shiga told his story of how he had found the lair one morning and Bruj had followed him—they had been asked not to talk about it—how people had only been warned about the she-wolf and not told of the pups.

Manuk nodded, "We didn't want any panic before First Hunt. We kept watch."

Shiga continued his story to tell them he had found them killed the afternoon the herd had been sighted and the signal fire lit.

"Anyone else could have found them," said Nad. "After all it was just below Mammoth Cliff." He looked at Shiga pointedly.

Shiga was silent. He would have to mention Hil—if only to absolve himself.

"We had forbidden anyone to go to the little wood—except the guards—Gath, Rit and Shiga." Tribe Mother spoke up, her eyes hard on Nad. This mistrust between tribes was uncommon.

Lith nodded.

Nad was quiet for a time. It would be pushing to imply doubt on the words of Tribe Mother of Healing Tree and Manuk.

Ina seemed about to say something , then thinking the better of it kept quiet.

"So you did not kill them!" Nad turned back to Shiga. Manuk shifted and Shiga looked at him. How would he or they prove—he would have to bring Hil into this. He tried again

"If I wanted to kill them, I could have done that earlier—before Manuk knew about them! And Hil—she has proof!"

He hated this—the more people it involved, the uglier it would get! But he had to clear his name—it seemed even saving Bruj's life had not absolved him.

Duk from the Tribe of Horse spoke up—they had all been silent allowing the tribes of Wolf and Tree to sort this out. But Duk felt it was time to intervene. For some time Nad's behaviour had been annoying them all. No wonder, he thought, young Bruj had been misled. "Can we call Hil, Manuk?"

Manuk strode out without a word and returned with Hil.

"Killing the totem makes one a cast-out," said Nad his eyes resting on Shiga, Bruj and now Hil in turn. "And endangering First Hunt" this time his flint-like eyes rested hard on Bruj. Ina put an arm around her brother.

Shiga looked at them and suddenly his heart was

filled with pity. He could have been there in Bruj's place if he had not joined First Hunt. It was funny! You could be cast out for not killing at a hunt and you could be cast out for killing at another time! It didn't make sense.

Murmured conversations broke out amongst the tribes. Shiga sought Manuk's eyes and asked for permission to speak. It was given with a nod.

"The wolf-pups would have died for lack of food, once the she-wolf was killed. Perhaps it was done as a favour…" his voice petered out, it sounded so lame.

Bruj was looking at him, his eyes blazing. He stood up.

"Sit down" Nad's voice roared, startling all. He turned towards Shiga and regarded him for a long while.

"Thank you."

Shiga was given permission to leave and he came out to find Urm waiting for him.

"How did it go?" he saw her anxiety.

Shiga just shook his head and they walked slowly towards the river-break.

Later they heard Bruj was not to be cast out—the

Tribe Mothers had pleaded on his behalf. But he was to spend two years in each tribe and was not allowed to return to his own before the next eight years had passed! And he was not allowed a mate in all that time!

The punishment was mainly for endangering First Hunt.

It was a hard punishment and Shiga felt he would have preferred to be an outcast. Eight years among people who looked down on you was worse.

Epilogue

Three large fires burnt on Lakeshore, keeping away the cold and the hyenas, but the noise of loud laughter and chatter and shouts were enough to keep them away. Children had been allowed to stay up but warned to stay close to the fires. Thrilled they gambolled around, while the quieter ones sat roasting some of the nuts their mothers and sisters had gathered; the babies were asleep in the women's hut, snug under the fur-covers with an old woman sitting watch in front of the low doorway.

"A wonderful meal," Gath rubbed his stomach.

"Hmm, especially that stew of perch and roots. It had a most lovely flavour to it," said Shiga.

"That was gogd, it's a herb which takes away the cold," said Urm sitting cross legged. A child lay asleep in front of her and she was ruffling his hair.

"Smells good too. Wish we had more salt though." Shiga eyes the little girl jealously and wished it was his hair she was ruffling. Since that hug she had given him and—and the kiss she had allowed Shiga could think of little else…

"The Horse Tribe didn't bring enough. They like to exchange it for things they need. No manners." Gath's tongue had loosened with rak—the parsnip drink. Urm and Shiga exchanged amused glances.

The fire blazed late into the cold night. All had gathered for the storytelling.

The Old Ones, said the wiry old woman, of the Tribe of Lake, pointing to Duni's red hair. Touching her hair Duni smiled self-consciously. The storytelling had begun.

The Old Ones, many of them had hair that colour. In

a land far from here—she pointed to the north west—
The land where the sun goes at nightfall. That is where
our first fathers and mothers lived. They were few and
life was hard. But it was not so cold so there was enough
to hunt. And gather. The Old Ones took their share of
the Goddess's gifts. But many did not like that.

She paused. A slow murmur passed through the
gathered people. It was an oft-repeated story.

The Old Ones looked different. They spoke differently—
using many grunts and clicks. Our ancestors held them
in scorn.

But Old Ones used fire and prayed to the Goddess
Mother. Like us. They knew the plants and trees—better
than us. The Old Ones kept away from us as much as
they could.

One late gathering time, a sickness came to the land.
It came to the Old Ones. Some of them were found
dead but it was not an animal that killed them. Their
bodies were swollen; no one had done the Otherworld
Ceremony. Yes, they had the ceremonies to send the
dead to the Otherworld—just like us.

A few of the older children shifted uncomfortably

until an adult hand touched them in comfort.

First it was one or two. Then more and more. Afraid, our forefathers stayed far from them. Some said Goddess Mother did not want the Old Ones. But that was not true. One or two who went near a dying one, caught the sickness and died. And so they were shunned or chased away to places where food was scarce.

A wolf howled far away. The fires were stoked higher.

When at last the sickness left, Freeze had come upon the land. Very few of the Old Ones survived the Freeze. For they lived away from the hunting grounds, away from their first homes, chased far north, where very little grew and the animals had left.

Chasing a fox one cold day, a hunter came across an Elder of the Old Ones. She was dying outside a tiny cave, where she lived alone. It wasn't the sickness but old age and loneliness.

He raised his spear to kill but some spirit stopped his hand. She was frail and her breath rattling, she was at the door of the Otherworld. Reluctantly the hunter brought her water and offered her food. She swallowed the water but refused to eat.

He paused. There was silence around the fires. A wind sprang up from Lake and the people drew their coats and fur blankets tighter.

Reluctantly, he sat beside her. He asked her why she had stayed.

"I am too old and my time is over," she panted, but "The Goddess's wrath will be upon the Tribe of Killers," she said with her dying breath.

Yes that is what the Old Ones called our ancestors.

The storyteller paused and lowered his head in remembered shame. His listeners did the same. After a while he lifted his head and with a sigh continued.

"My people will find a better place. But this land of the Killer Tribe will change. You too will be driven away. Just like us".

Then the Old One died.

Frightened, the hunter returned to his people and told them of the incident. Many laughed. But some knew they had done great wrong. And felt a deep fear. A special ceremony was planned to appease the Goddess.

But that night, the hill near the land where the forefathers lived made strange noises—grumbling and growling like a cave lion. The next day there was smoke.

For a few days the hill continued to rumble. Smoke bellowed out of its top like a huge fire. People talked of leaving. The special Ceremony was completed hastily.

Again she paused.

Shiga found his heart beating a little faster—he heard the Old Story often and yet—he reached out for Urm's warm hand.

But Goddess Mother was not pleased. The hill continued to rumble and grumble.

Then one night, it vomited a large fireball, which rolled down the hill to their cave. People ran in terror. When they fell, the fire caught up with them and turned them to rock.

Three days and three nights the hill belched fire. The sky remained dark even at dawn. The sun did not visit the land. Ashes covered everything—it buried the plants and grasses; animals had either run away or were dead. Nothing lived.

The hunter had found shelter in the very cave outside which he had found the Old One. When the hill had quietened, he came out to look for his people. There was no one—just dead buried in ashes.

At last he came across a little girl and her mother hanging onto the branches of a large tree. The Tree had been spared from the fire, though ash covered half its bole. He brought them to the cave, shared his small pouch of food, but what kept them alive was a spring inside that tiny cave—its waters still ran clear.

Together they searched—but saw only terrible sights. Mothers and babies, old men and women, children—all turned into black rock. Frozen by fire and ash in the very place they had fallen. Only two were alive. They brought them back.

A deep sigh passed through the gathered listeners. Far away a hyena cackled. The fire was low and Shiga threw a log onto it. It spluttered and the silent group sat up, startled. The storyteller began again.

The land gave no food. The little stream near their home was half submerged in ash. They had no spears or tools to hunt with and could find no stones or bones to make one. Besides there were no animals. Then the hunter said they must travel—away from the land where the Mother Goddess had spent her anger, away from where they had done so great a wrong.

"We must go," said he, "to a place where we can live and hunt again. And gather. We must revere the Tree and the Mother. Never again should we kill the Mother's creatures without cause." They agreed and the long journey began.

"And then we reached here," whispered Urm.

Yes we reached here but it was after a long, hard journey of many moons and suns, said the storyteller, as if she had heard her.

When we reached this land, the hunter saw Tree. No one had seen anything so big. They sheltered there for many moons and found her providing fruit and strength.

"It is a sign from the Goddess," he said. "She has forgiven us and this is where we will live. We will be the Tribe of Healing Tree, we will heal before we hurt."

As time went by the hunter and the woman he'd saved had children, many children. Some went to establish other tribes. And a few peoples came from other lands and joined the tribes.

"And that is how Tribes of today came to be here," finished the storyteller. "And we are all children of these fore-fathers. And so too Tribe of Healing Tree is the oldest."

"We have been careful to follow the wishes of the Earth Goddess, who is the Mother of all human and animal. The tribe has grown and learnt. But as the Old One said, this land is hard and grows harsher as if the Mother Goddess is tired and needs a long sleep. That is why we have colder Freezes but we follow her laws and live.

"And some of us have red hair. It is a sign and a reminder from the Mother. Of the Old Ones who live no more but through us. Some say that the very First Healer was an Old One," he shook his head at the great mystery. "Much of what we know and do is learnt from them. But most of all we have learnt to live in peace."

There was silence for a while. A snow owl hooted in the woods, preparing for its night hunt. People coughed and moved their limbs. One or two stood up and stretched. The night was warm. The wind had dropped. It was time for the announcements of Joining.

Shiga sat at the edge of the group. He turned to look across the waters towards the dark shape of the woods. Above him the sky was like a black meadow- its star flowers glittering. From the corner of his eye he saw Tribe Mothers move up near the middle fire. They talked softly among themselves. A soft murmur broke.

It was the norm of the couples to approach their Tribe Mothers for permission to join. Rarely was it refused. But this was all done before the Joinings were announced to the gathered tribes. He turned towards Urm, then panicked. She had disappeared. How had he missed her leaving? Had she really agreed to join him? He saw Lup and Hil move up hand in hand. Then he heard Tribe Mother call his name.

Shiga stood up feeling foolish. Then he saw Urm. Coming out of the hut. She was dressed in the soft hares' skin coat and trousers she had made last

Growing. From hareskins that had been his gift to her. On her hair she wore the red fox tail band. The fox that he had hunted. She smiled at him as she moved toward the fire. She looked so beautiful!

His heart couldn't seem to steady, and his ears went as red as the foxtail. Someone thumped him on the back and urged him on.

As he stood by Urm facing the Tribe Mothers, his mother—Tribe Mother of Healing Tree smiled at them. The firelight danced on Urm's hair and face. In the dark night a hush fell on the tribes. Shiga thought he was being given a tree spirit as his mate. He heard Tribe Mother saying their names. He heard little else for a cheering broke from Gath and Manuk and Riv and Roni and his friend Rit, even the children.

Holding Urm's hand, Shiga went to sit with the new Joiners. There were a few other Joinings to be announced.

People were retiring to sleep what remained of the night. Some sat talking together. Rit was talking earnestly to Ina, who still looked glum. And Shiga turned back to Lake. He and Urm sat side by side a little away, looking over the waters. Though it would be some time before their joining in the late Growing, Shiga felt a confidence that he had not felt before.

He was no longer afraid to hunt big game, though he would never enjoy it like other hunters. But he had learnt to put the tribe first. He wondered about the Old Ones and felt sad. The Freezes were bad, but he could face anything, if Urm was by him. And he would help Urm to grow food and one day they would be able to tell people about it.

Shiga gave a deep sigh and looked up at the cold blue star over Lake. Urm leaned her head onto his shoulder and a gentle breeze rose wrapping around them. In silence they thanked Goddess Mother.

Author's Note

The last Ice Age began about 110,000 years ago and ended about 12,500 years ago. Glaciers covered most of the earth, the continents were larger. Where there are seas today, lands were joined—like the Bering Sea and the Persian Gulf.

The continent of Asia and Europe (Eurasia) was larger. Humans led very different lives. They had to be adaptable, strong and make whatever they needed from the natural world.

People followed and hunted—mammoths, bison, giant deer, elk and other large Ice Age animals. In the short summers they gathered fruits, tubers, plants for medicines and food.

About 13,000 years ago there was a sudden very cold

phase—just before the present, warmer ice-less climate (Holocene) set in.

Called the Younger Dryas it was less pronounced in the southeast of the Asian continent. In the area which is northern Mongolia, China and southern Siberia many wildlife took refuge; and people followed. Except in the high mountains the land was glacier free and people lived there on river terraces and valleys. The ice and glaciers had also created many lakes in these regions providing fish and freshwater.

The Game Hunters is set in this landscape.

The vast Eurasian steppe lands had long severe winters (–45 degrees) and short summers. Trees were few and mostly grew in their dwarf varieties, near lakes there could be small woods. The summer grass brought the herbivorous animals to graze and people prepared areas where they could hunt them after fencing them in. Bison and deer were hunted in this way.

Mammoth population had decreased—due to changing climate and also because of extensive hunting.

People lived in tribes. The cold snap probably forced them to adapt by changing their ways of living and hunting even more. Food shortage and starvation were not uncommon. Populations dwindled. A good hunt was essential to survival.

Hunting big game required immense cooperation, patience and trust in each other. So Shiga's refusal to hunt would have been a very serious matter.

Hunting was also dangerous and growing from childhood to 'hunter' status would require transformation rituals- like Shiga's initiation.

It is still practised in the hunter-gatherer societies of today.

Hunting and tool-making were also skills to be learnt, probably as an apprentice to a master toolmaker and senior hunters.

Quick gathering in summer of necessary plants and fruits would provide the vital balance to a primary diet of meat, as well as medicines for sicknesses. This required a thorough knowledge of the local environment—of climate, plants, Nature.

Observant gatherers were sure to notice that seeds and seedlings near water-bodies thrived well; maybe someone discovered that if the plants were cared for they did even better. Agriculture came much later but anthropologists and archaeologists tell us that nurturing wild plants must have happened in various places.

Urm notices this but taboos to 'tampering with Nature' forces her to keep her knowledge secret.

In Palaeolithic life, the inter-dependency of animal, Nature and man was respected. Objects of Nature held special significance (e.g. a single large tree growing in a treeless icy plain) as did the colour red—used in rituals and cave painting.

The earth was mother and goddess—rejuvenating herself each year—bringing forth fresh life every spring and summer.

Underground caves in many Asian cultures hold significance as places of 'feminine' earth energy. Most prehistoric cave paintings are found in deep caves; it is quite likely that there were pre-hunting rituals to invoke the bounty of the Earth Goddess in secret underground chambers.

Paleolithic people had a rich culture of music, drawing, and rituals just like us.

Women as mothers likely held a high position in prehistoric society. They were also caregivers and healers and had a deep knowledge of local medicines and were leaders of tribes.

In the entire context of Ice Age societies tribes would be more important than individual freedom—as survival depended on mutual cooperation.

We humans are social beings.

Early research on prehistory focused on Europe. In recent years discovery of the 40 thousand-year-old Indonesian cave drawings, the Denisovan branch of the human family—all show that the south-eastern region of continental Asia was home to a rich Palaeolithic culture over 55 thousand years old. It is our common ancestry; for much of culture, society and human behaviour was born of our life in the Ice Age.

The Game Hunters is a 'prehistoric fiction'—a story

both about breaking traditions and putting others before self.

For more information on the Ice Age—see my blog article—*Sculpted by Ice* (https://anuparoy.wordpress.com).

Notes for the four illustrations:

pp. 11, 17, 27, 41
Figurines from Mal'ta-Buret prehistoric sites, carved from mammoth-ivory, probably used as pendants, 20,000 years old

pp. 53, 65, 79
Serpent images from Mal'ta-Buret, could have ritualistic use

pp. 89, 107, 123
Flying snow geese figure from Mal'ta-Buret, pendant(?), 18,000 years old

pp. 137, 147, 167, 177, 191
Bison cow figure from Zaraysk prehistoric site in Russia, carved from mammoth-ivory, was used for ritual, 20,000 years old

Further Reading

To read more about Ice Age people and times:

The Art of the Ice Age.
http://www.bradshawfoundation.com/sculpture/

Prehistoric Map.
http://prehistoricmap.com/

Hans Berekoven, "The Ice Age and its effect on Human Migration."
https://www.maritimemysteries.org/the-ice-age-and-its-effect-on-human-migration.html

Mark Prigg, "How the world looked during the last Ice Age."
http://www.dailymail.co.uk/sciencetech/article-2630738/

Chris Scarre, *The Human Past, 4th Edition* (London: Thames & Hudson 2018).

"Tales set in stone." *A World of Science* Vol 10, No.3 (2012).
http://unesdoc.unesco.org/images/0021/002171/217154E.pdf

Anupa Roy is a writer and librarian. Her deepest interests lie in exploring how history in a geographical context shapes a culture and its people; she uses this to explore the human relationship to Nature in her writings and readings. Her first forays in children's publishing were two picture books titled—*Travels of Little Rice Grass* and *Travels of Little Tea Leaves*.